MW01133730

WITHDRAWN

A Little
Taste of
Heaven

DOREEN RAWLINS

WESTBOW
PRESS®
A DIVISION OF THOMAS NELSON
& ZONDERVAN

WestBow Press books may be ordered through booksellers or by contacting:

WestBow Press
A Division of Thomas Nelson & Zondervan
1663 Liberty Drive
Bloomington, IN 47403
www.westbowpress.com
1 (866) 928-1240

ISBN: 978-1-5127-5311-0 (sc)
ISBN: 978-1-5127-5312-7 (hc)
ISBN: 978-1-5127-5310-3 (e)

Library of Congress Control Number: 2016913216

Print information available on the last page.

WestBow Press rev. date: 09/13/2016

This story is dedicated to my grandsons, Ross and Reed Rawlins. Twins. Identical, inseparable, and unpredictable schemers. Growing up on an Oregon cattle ranch, they stacked mountains of firewood, working side by side in matching coveralls, starting around age four. They would spend hours in the shop, creating a horse-drawn thingamabob and then go flying by the kitchen window, one holding on for dear life, the other running the horse full speed. Even though they are part of a big family, those two had their own agenda, plotting and planning. The rest of us wondered, "What are they up to now?" There's just something uniquely amazing about twins. Love you, twinners!

Part One

KATE

*"Be strong and courageous! Do not be terrified or dismayed,
for the Lord your God is with you wherever you go."*
Joshua 1:9

Chapter 1

The Wells Fargo stage stop was a welcome respite from the last two days of hard travel. More of an inn, the charming, whitewashed, two-story building had lace curtains in the windows along the front—a woman's touch. A stone fireplace burned cheerfully, warming the long, narrow room. Rag rugs on polished wood floors gave a homey feel, and tables with unmatched chairs were kept spotless, set up for the next group of weary travelers.

Sitting across from her father, Clayton, with a cup of hot coffee, Kate began to feel confident again. She had known her decision to take him to Oregon was the right thing, and she felt surer now than ever. The hostess, Millie Thatcher, a sturdy type, approached their table with a gracious smile, her deep-blue eyes sparkling. She served a plate of warm bread, a crock of butter, and deep bowls of hearty beef stew.

Kate waited for the delicious-smelling stuff to cool a bit and then gently encouraged her father to take a bite. Indicating with her own bite, she said, "This way, Papa." Were he in his right mind, Kate knew her father would be appalled that he could no longer perform ordinary tasks. "Here, Papa, try this." She slathered creamy butter on a slice of bread and handed it to him. After he mindlessly studied it, he carefully tore the bread into bits, dropping the pieces one at a time into his stew. And then, as if it were customary, he dolloped berry preserves over the whole kit and caboodle and dug in.

Kate glanced around, but no one seemed to notice. Whether or not it made a bit of difference to her father, she tore her own bread into pieces and topped her stew as well. As for the preserves, that's where she drew the line.

Early the next morning, with the passengers revived, rested, and satisfied with a bountiful breakfast, it was time to load up for the next leg of travel. A fresh team of horses had been hitched up and was raring to go. Kate tucked Clayton's right hand in the crook of her arm, and a walking stick in his left kept the old man upright as they shuffled slowly toward the coach. Her travel bag was scrunched under her other arm. She was feeling renewed and encouraged that she was doing the right thing. She felt a contentment she hadn't felt in ages.

Suddenly, like a Kansas thunderbolt, shots rang out. Screams pierced the air as stage-stop patrons scrambled for cover. From behind Kate, a strong, rough arm drew her in a vice-like grip, and Clayton fell to the ground. The smell of sweat and whiskey assaulted her nostrils, and she felt the cold barrel of a pistol pressed against her temple. Another gunman appeared atop the stagecoach and held the group of terrified travelers frozen in place.

"Ain't nobody move, or the lady gets it!" He fired above their heads for added effect, spit a stream of tobacco through a gap in his teeth, and laughed harshly. Kate struggled to get free, stabbing with her elbows and kicking furiously, but to no avail. The sweaty outlaw dragged her, kicking and screaming, toward the coach.

"Let go of me, you dirty yella-belly polecat. *Let me go!* Right now, ya lowdown sidewinder! My papa needs help.—Help!" As the door slammed shut on the hem of her dress, the stagecoach jerked to a start. Kate's muffled, sobbing pleas grew faint— "Somebody please help my papa"—until she could no longer be heard. There was nothing on the horizon but dust, and the ring of warning shots grew fainter and fainter.

Silas had his pistol in one hand, aimed at Kate, and his filthy canteen full of moonshine in the other. Everything about him was filthy dirty. Sweat streaked the dust on his face, making him appear way beyond his fifty-some years. Even *he* didn't know for sure how old he was. He kept one eye out the window and one on her, which was easy, since he was cockeyed—born that way, he figured. His filthy dirty hat was pulled down hard on his filthy dirty head.

Kate sat across from him in the far corner, sniffling in her white lace hanky. Silas took a long swig from the canteen and then another; it burned all the way to his gullet. The jolting of the coach and effects of the whiskey soon had him feeling drowsy. His eyelids grew heavier and heavier. The gun slipped a bit from its target, and finally toppled to the floor. Kate jumped at the sound, but Silas—now passed out—didn't hear it.

Kate reached it with the tip of her toe and gingerly slid it closer and closer—then just a little bit closer. Silas snorted. She froze. The pistol was now hidden by her skirts. All she had to do was reach down and—he snorted again. She froze again. Keeping her eyes on him, she retrieved the six-shooter slowly, concealing it under the folds of her traveling dress. She had it!

Kate's eyes grew big at the realization that now she had the upper hand. She was no longer the hostage—Silas was. And she knew how to shoot a gun. Her father had taught his four daughters how to survive in rugged Kansas rangeland—and he'd taught them well. He always boasted that Kate could shoot a can off the fencepost from a mile away. Of course, shooting a tin can was one thing. Could she shoot a man? Even if that man was a filthy, dirty, cockeyed outlaw? She knew for sure she couldn't.

Kate looked at Silas's filthy boots. Maybe if she just shot off a toe or two, it would slow him down so she could escape. But then the other mangy outlaw would have to be dealt with. She was in a terrible predicament; she had to get away and get back to her father. She knew he was probably frantic, not knowing where she was or even where *he* was. No one would know how to care for him. No one loved him like Kate.

Even her sisters had wanted to put the old man in an asylum. But that would not happen. Kate would make sure of it. By then, her three self-absorbed sisters would have discovered she'd packed up her and Clayton's belongings and left. She assumed that none of them would even care. More likely, they would rejoice to have the place all to themselves.

Kate began to pray, "Oh Lord, please help me. I'm in a terrible scrape here." Out of nowhere, a Scripture verse came to her mind— one she memorized after her mother died. Kate was only seven at the time, but through the years that verse from the book of Joshua had helped her in times of loneliness and need. *Be strong and of good courage; be not frightened, neither be dismayed; for the Lord your God is with you wherever you go.* Kate closed her eyes and thought about those words of truth; she thought about how her mother read them from the family Bible and sang hymns to her so many years ago. She could almost hear her mama's voice.

Kate began to hum and then softly sing. "Amazing grace, how sweet the sound that saved a wretch like me. I once was lost but now I'm found, was blind but now I see." Her sweet voice grew stronger as she became lost in the wondrous grace of Jesus. "'Twas grace that taught my heart to fear, and grace my fear re—"

Suddenly her reverie was shattered as Silas blew his nose and swiped at his eyes. *Was that a tear?* she wondered. Silas scrambled, looking for his pistol. Kate couldn't stop staring. *I think he was crying.*

He mumbled some choice words under his breath, searched behind him, searched the floor, and then looked across at her. "You see my gun?"

"It's in my pocket," Kate replied, glancing toward her right hand, also in that pocket.

He shrugged, not bothered much that she had the gun. He was quiet and then said, "My ma used to sing that there song in church." He looked down.

"You've been to church?" she asked in disbelief.

"Yep. Raised up goin' ta church, me and my brothers." Silas seemed to take on a different countenance. She could almost picture him as a little boy. "Never knew my pa," he went on, "and when Ma died, us boys quit goin'. Didn't seem right since we was havin' ta steal just ta eat. Ya knows what I mean? Goin' to church and stealin', that ain't right."

Kate felt a bit of compassion. "So you know about Jesus? You know about forgiveness?"

Silas slowly nodded, and looking straight in her eyes—as well as he could in his condition—said, "Yes, ma'am. I been dunked in the river even."

"You've been baptized?" She leaned forward, the look on her face radiant. "Praise the Lord! This is wonderful news. You don't need to live this outlaw life you been livin'. You're a child of the King! Praise the Lord! Thank you, Jesus! Oh – and here's your gun back."

———

They had talked and prayed together for at least an hour when the coach began to climb a mountain pass, slowing from the furious pace they had endured since leaving the stagecoach stop— and leaving her father. Silas had repented and asked the Lord for forgiveness; he was a changed man before her very eyes, by God's amazing grace.

Silas looked out the window, surveying the area—searching ahead, looking back, and looking up to gauge the time. "We'll be comin' to a spot up ahead, maybe half-hour away, where ya best try to escape, ma'am. Boss will be concentratin' on gettin' this thang down a steep dip and round a curve at the same time. He'll be lookin' to the left and drivin' slow. If ya time it just right, you can jump out the right-side door into a gulley of moss and ferns. Shouldn't bung ya up too bad."

Kate had been so caught up in the miracle that had happened, she'd nearly forgotten the need to escape. "But what good would that do?" she asked Silas. "We've traveled a long distance—too far to make it back to my father before dark. Could I even survive out here all night? And what about you?"

Silas didn't hesitate. "Trust me, Miss Kate, you want to be gone before Boss gets to our hideout, where we stash the loot. He's crazy. No tellin' what he's a mind to. Your chances are better out here with bears and wildcats. Sides, I'll be prayin' the Lord put a legion a' angels round ya. I'll be prayin' for your protection."

"But what about you?" she asked again, this time with tears spilling over.

"Well, I reckon you'll be prayin' for me too." He pointed to her travel bag. "You'll wanta have a tight hold on that thang when ya jump. And here—might as well put this in there too." Silas handed back the pistol.

Kate composed herself, trying to build up courage to jump from the moving coach into the complete unknown. Again she quoted Joshua 1:9 as she clutched her bag and held tightly to the doorframe. Silas was next to her, ready to release the door, which would swing open on its own accord, since it was hinged on the downhill side.

She couldn't do it, but she had to do it. Before she could change her mind, Silas kissed her on the head and then kicked her on the backside. "God bless ya, sweet angel."

———

The sun had slid behind tall pines when Kate blinked and touched the side of her head. She tried to sit up. *Where am I?* Her hair felt matted on one side, just above her ear—and sticky. She glanced about and saw the contents of her traveling bag scattered in every direction. Dizzy, her head throbbing, she collapsed back and closed her eyes against the pain; slowly remembering bits and pieces: *Silas, the stagecoach. Papa!*

Kate forced herself to rise up on her elbows. She surveyed the articles from her bag: two combs, two pistols, two of everything. Struggling to raise up on her left elbow, she felt the knot on her head again and recognized that the stickiness was dried blood. The ditch where she'd landed seemed a carpet of lush green moss, just as Silas described. Except for that one rock, the one that evidently knocked her for a loop. Forcing herself to hands and knees, Kate tediously began to gather her belongings, two by two.

Oh Lord, please help me! I've got to get back to Papa. Protect him, Lord, and give me wisdom. She thought about her father being alone in a strange place, probably frightened and looking frantically for his dear Kate. She too was lost and alone in a strange place. It was growing dark, her head was pounding, and she was seeing double. She decide it had been very bad judgement after all, taking her father to Oregon. She wondered if she would ever see him again. *Oh Lord, what have I done?*

Katherine Lee Alexander was only nineteen years old, but she felt the weight of the world on her shoulders.

Chapter 2

Jeremiah Maxwell Reed was twenty years old and felt the weight of the world on his shoulders too. There he was, broke down in the middle of nowhere, having the sole responsibility for his little brothers and growing low on supplies, which had tumbled from their disabled wagon. He somehow had known the axel was about to break just before it happened. He had slowed the mules, but not in time to avoid the back wheels pitching over the edge of a deep gully, splitting the old wagon in two. Their earthly goods had spilled out all over tarnation.

Sampson and Delilah, the mules, were braying frantically. Max quickly unhitched them and hollered at the boys to lead them to a stream just beyond their scattered belongings. He led the horses and followed, surveying the area with a clear knowledge: this is where they would spend the night or maybe two, until he figured out how to remedy the predicament they were in.

It took most the afternoon to set up camp and haul their trunks and crates—at least those not shattered on impact—to a safe place. Bags of grain and beans, flour and sugar had busted open; patched-up hand-me-downs were scattered about; tools, pots, and pans lay in a heap; and their mother's trunk was in the middle of the mess, still closed and thankfully in one piece. Luckily they discovered a small cave that would serve as a shelter for their meager possessions.

Max tipped his hat back and swiped a shirtsleeve across his forehead, trying to keep sweat out of his eyes. He looked over at Josh and Joey, sweating just as much, working hard with not a complaint. They were good boys, nine years old. *Been through a lot those two.* Max realized that if they had to break down, at least it was a good spot with water nearby and a bit of shelter. He tried to convince himself that this mishap would not derail their plans to make it to Oregon before bad weather set in.

Max was as determined as his father had been to find a better life in Oregon. He remembered out loud what his father had said: "Land of my own, a ranch, cattle—the land of milk and honey." But his father's dreams would never come to pass.

———

Max's mother had died giving birth to him, and when he was three, his father decided the two of them would leave Missouri and head west. They got as far as the Casey Ranch in eastern Wyoming, where Max's father was hired on for a branding by Ruth Casey, a young widow and owner of the ranch. She had lost her husband and child in a house fire. A blackened stone fireplace was the only vestige.

Ruth took to little Max right off, and Max, longing for a mother, loved Ruth. Eventually, his father saw the light and asked Ruth for her hand in marriage. Even though it was an arrangement out of necessity—her needing a man to manage the ranch and him needing a mother for his son—Jeremiah and Ruthie Reed eventually fell in love. Dreams of Oregon Country were set aside, and father and son worked the Wyoming ranch, grateful at the end of each day when Ruth welcomed them home to a bountiful supper.

When Max turned eleven, to his utter amazement and delight, Ruth gave birth to twin boys. The cabin his father had built suddenly was bustling with busyness. For a while, the ladies of Hope Church came out from town in pairs to cook and wash and help care for the babies, Joseph and Joshua. But eventually Max went from ranch-hand to housekeeper. He genuinely loved helping his mother, the only one he'd ever known, with the boys. They were truly a blessed and happy family.

Then, when the boys were five, suddenly Ruth became critically ill and died. Their father buried her in a grave behind Hope Church. He was never the same after that. His own health began to fail, and though he tried to muster up courage to talk about Oregon again, he couldn't seem to pull out of the dark place that consumed him. Three years later, they buried him next to Ruth, behind Hope Church.

In his despair, their father had let the ranch go. Their cow herd had dwindled; the pastures, once lush, were overgrown with ragweed. The old barn leaned as if tired of standing straight. When the banker showed up one cold April morning to deliver foreclosure papers, Max made a decision. He would pick up where his father had left off seventeen years before. He and the boys were going to Oregon.

———

The shadows grew long as Kate struggled to make her way uphill, deeper into the forest, stopping from tree to tree to steady herself. Her head felt like it was splitting, and she had gone without water since early morning. Dizziness got hold of her; she closed her eyes, leaning into a huge pine. *Lord, please point me in the right direction. Give me strength, let me—*

What was that? It sounded to her like a horse whinnying. She thought it must be her head injury. *Wait.* She heard it again—a voice, almost inaudible. *Is that someone talking? Laughing?*

With fear and hope, she followed the sound to a ledge about thirty feet above a grassy meadow with a stream winding through it. Kate could barely see in the shade of cottonwood trees, but sure enough, tied there was a horse, grazing. Straining to hear hushed voices, she took another step. She knew they must be directly below her. One more step. Shale began sliding beneath her feet, and for the second time that day, Kate was hurling to the ground, clutching her travel bag as if it could save her.

At the sound of a yelp and of shale flying in all directions, Max looked up to see a flurry of petticoats heading right toward him. He instinctively braced himself, arms outstretched, and caught her. The impact knocked him on his rump. When the dust settled, Max, with eyes wide, mouth open, and in a state of disbelief, was holding the prettiest little thing he'd ever laid eyes on.

Slowly her eyes opened—soft hazel eyes with long black lashes— her skin was like cream. Their faces were just inches apart. With a shaky voice, she said, "Please, sir. Please put me down. Please." *Polite too,* he thought as she wrestled out of his hold and tried to stand, which didn't go well. Max also stood and grasped her arm as she swayed, suddenly looking very pale.

Kate tried desperately to collect herself, and then she saw them. Two sets of brown eyes, two sets of shaggy blond hair. It was happening again. She was seeing double. And at that moment she collapsed, out cold, back into Max's arms.

Max directed the boys to lay out his bed roll and get a fire started. Kate was limp as a rag as he gently lay her down, careful of what appeared to be a head wound. Soon all three brothers were on their knees, staring down at her face.

"Is she gonna die?" Josh asked.

"Her pulse is strong. I think she just needs rest," Max replied.

"Thee thur ith purty, Maxth," Joey said.

"Quit talkin' baby talk, Joey!" Josh chided.

With a stern look, Max admonished, "Let him be, Joshua." Whenever Max said *Joshua* or *Joseph,* the boys knew he meant business. Each twin had taken the loss of their mother in different ways: Josh got tougher and Joey more melancholy. Max empathized with both.

The sky was growing rich with sunset colors, pinks and purples, fading into the gray of dusk. It was time for supper, such as it was. Their "guest" was still out, so Max sent the boys in search of a quilt he remembered might be in their mother's trunk. He could hear them chattering excitedly inside the cave, as if they had found a great treasure. And then, "Max! C'mere. We found it!"

"The quilt?"

"Yes, but somethin else too. Somethin better!" Max ducked to enter the cave, just as they came charging out, shouting in unison, "Mama's Bible, Max! We found her Bible. We thought it was long gone, remember?"

———

Except for the glow of firelight, it was pitch dark. The boys seemed to be having a hard time settling down. Max couldn't quite decipher their whispers, but there was no mistaking the giggles. "Quiet now, boys. Go to sleep. Tomorrow'll be a long day." Laughter continued, and their attempt to smother their voices in a shared pillow was a lost cause. "What are you two talkin' about, anyway?"

"Oh, nothing", they said in unison, a little too quickly.

Max got up from where he was trying to read in the fire's glow. He lumbered to their side and stood tall above their bedroll. "C'mon. What's so funny?"

That question made them laugh all the more. Josh, trying to get himself together, spoke first. "Remember, Max, the time Pa said— *giggle, giggle*—you needed to be lookin' for a good wife?"

Then Joey jumped in. "And you thed—*giggle, giggle, giggle*—if God wanted you to have a wife, He'd have ta drop her in your lap. Well, guesth what?"

The boys were sitting up by then and together said, "He just did!" They fell back on their pillow, holding their sides for laughing so hard. Max couldn't help but laugh himself.

The commotion didn't disturb Kate one bit. She was still sleeping soundly. Something did awaken, however, in the deep place of Max's heart.

———

Kate stirred in the night air, a quilt tucked under her chin, smelling of musty lavender as if it was timeworn and had been stored with lavender sachets. A fire was burning low to her left. She lifted her head from a makeshift pillow just enough to realize it hurt like thunder and began to slowly remember what had happened. The stagecoach robbery, Silas, jumping, falling, and—*Papa.*

She sat up. On the other side of the fire, two small forms were snuggled together in one bedroll, their hair disheveled and their faces dirty. At least she wasn't still suffering from double vision. The young boys were facing each other. Someone was to her right, leaning against the rock wall, his hat tipped down, arms folded across his broad chest, boots crossed. His rifle was propped at the ready next to him; a pistol was tucked in his belt. *He must be the one that caught me.*

Kate looked up into the velvet sky, a blanket of bright stars blinking back at her. *Thank you, Lord. You heard my prayer and answered me. You saved me, Lord, in a most miraculous way. Surely I'm safe with these strangers.* She looked again at the young man trying to sleep against hard cold rock. There was a book on his lap she hadn't noticed before. The fire flared up, and for a moment she could clearly see gold letters: *Holy Bible.*

Chapter 3

The smell of coffee woke Kate for the second time, and she sat up slowly and stretched. Three pairs of deep-brown eyes were fixed on her. Instinctively, she touched the goose egg on the side of her head. A gentle voice said, "Can I take a look at that, ma'am?"

"Oh, uh," Kate stammered. "It's nothing. I must have hit my head on a rock when I jumped from the stagecoach. Actually, Silas booted me out, but he didn't expect there would be a rock."

Max scratched his head. "Must have been a pretty bad day, from the sound of things."

"Well, yes, really an awful day, except the part where Silas repented. Oh, I do hope he's all right. And all my things are still on the stage, probably stashed in Boss's hiding place. That's where they keep their loot, ya know? And my papa. Well, he has a memory problem, and he really needs me. I may never see him again." She burst into tears.

Joey poured some strong, hot coffee in a tin cup and brought it over to her. "Drink thith thtuff, ma'am. It'll do ya a world of good." It was the worst-tasting coffee Kate had ever experienced, but as she drank, warmth filled her from head to toe. And her tears subsided.

Josh came to her with a piece of jerky and a cold biscuit in a rusty skillet. It was more like a petrified biscuit. Kate smiled up at the two matching boys and then lowered her head and quietly gave thanks to the Lord.

They talked over breakfast, trading names and figuring out they were all bound for Oregon. Max said, "Once I get this wagon patched up, you'd be welcome to travel with us, Miss Kate."

She replied, "That's mighty kind of you, sir, but I must get back to my father at the stage stop. I'm able to pay for a ride." She patted her thighs nonchalantly to make sure the gold coins were still there, sewn into her pantaloons. "It's only about a day of travel," she added. Then, after a look at the state of their wagon, she added, "Maybe two."

"Ma'am, I'm already behind schedule as far as beatin' the weather. I can take you to the next town, where you could catch the stagecoach goin' back."

Kate diplomatically changed the subject. "Would you mind if the boys accompany me to the river? I would like to wash my face." Josh and Joey each grabbed a bucket and happily walked with Miss Kate, one on each side, down to the river.

In the meantime, Max started gathering his meager tools to begin work on their wagon, the two halves of which he and the boys had dragged to a level area. A saw would have helped, but all he had was a hammer and a bag of spilled nails.

Max knew it was going to be a hot day. He had worked up a sweat, and he started to wonder what was taking the boys and Kate so long. Just as he was about to go fetch them, he heard laughter coming from some ways off. He smiled, glad for the fun they were having, probably splashing each other from the riverbank. But he felt it was time that they get back to helping him with the wagon.

Their voices closer now, he could tell Kate was playing some kind of game with them. And around the corner they came: all three laughing, with scrubbed faces and hair washed and combed. Parted even.

Max had never seen the twins shined up like that. And Kate was glowing, her soft hair hanging down her back like silk.

"Max!" Josh exclaimed. "Look what we got!"

Max turned. "Did ya catch some frogs?"

"Berries. Miss Kate's gonna cook us a pie."

"That would be real nice, but our flour and sugar bags broke open, if you remember, only yesterday."

Josh and Joey looked at each other, knowing without a word what the other was thinking. They ran for the cave and after a minute or two came out holding some tins. "Sister Hildebrand packed these in Mama's trunk. Said it was a gift from the church for when we got to Oregon."

"Thith one ith flour, thith one thugar," added Joey.

"Perfect!" exclaimed Kate. "If we only had some lard." The boys nearly knocked each other over running back into the cave.

"Got it. Lard."

"And a little jar of thinnamon."

Max hadn't seen his brothers that happy in ages.

Kate tied her hair back and got to work. Before long, the heavenly aroma of berry cobbler filled the air, making everyone's mouth water with anticipation. She made a meal as best she could with what she found, with the promise of baked beans and fresh biscuits the next day. But she made it clear that was only if everyone pitched in after supper and picked up the scattered beans so she could wash and put them to soak.

Max had made some headway on the wagon, and he was hoping for better progress in the morning. Josh and Joey, with berry juice running down their chins, seemed to be in a private conversation, whispering, snickering, looking over their shoulder every little bit. Max was sure they were up to something, probably persuading Kate to make more cobblers.

He had to admit that she had cooked up a mighty fine cobbler, all sugary and sweet. She was pretty sweet too: good to the boys and pretty as a picture. *Settle down, Max,* he told himself, trying to get his mind on the goal at hand: fixing the wagon and getting back on the trail to Oregon.

The boys were sleeping, contented. Max and Kate sat by the fire, sipping somewhat better-tasting coffee, since Kate had thoroughly washed the pot. Their conversation easy, they talked about the boys mostly—how much alike they were and yet different.

When their mother died, Max told Kate, Joshua had become very angry; he was mad all the time. One time their colt kicked him in the rear, and Josh turned around and kicked him back. He never wanted to be with Max or Pa, not even Joey. Pa knew Christmas would be tough, so he special ordered the boys their own blade. He told them they needed to be menfolk and taught them how to throw. Max painted a big target on the side of the barn so they could practice. Josh tried for a while, but he lost interest and gave it up altogether. Joey just kept on practicing. Every day for hours, he threw that blade.

A few months went by with Josh continuing to ignore Joey, who was terribly hurt by it. One day, Pa sent them out to the back field to look for a lost calf. Josh figured they could spot it better from atop an expanse of rocks on the far end. Of course, he was trekking way ahead of Joe, keeping his usual distance. Nearing the rocks, Josh heard it before he saw it—a rattlesnake. He froze, stricken with fear, not knowing what to do. In the next instant, *thwap*! From somewhere behind him, Joey had thrown his blade, making a precise hit to the snake's head, killing it instantly.

That night at supper, Joshua had blurted out, "Joe saved my life today," and broke down, his head in his hands, sobbing. Joey didn't know how to react, so he started crying too. Max had been dishing up stew and stopped mid-scoop, overcome with emotion himself. He heard Pa sniff and blow his nose, trying to restrain his own emotions. "Let's say grace," he finally declared, and they bowed their heads. From then on, Josh and Joe, more than ever before, were inseparable.

Kate's own eyes pooled with empathy for the twin boys, as they had lost their mother so young. She could share their pain, having lost her own. And in a way, she was losing her father too—slowly, little by little. "There is so much we don't understand," she said to Max. "I guess we won't this side of heaven. But I do believe with all my heart that God dearly loves Josh and Joey and has a plan for their lives. He loves you too, Max, and me. We have to put our trust in Him."

She stared into the black night beyond the fire, as if her thoughts were miles away. "I prayed and believed I was doing the right thing, taking Papa to Oregon, with his dream being to go west, to find his brothers, Clete and Charlie. Even if that happens, he may not even know them anymore." She could no longer hold back the tears.

Max shifted, put his arm around her shoulder, and pulled her close. He comforted her with gentle words, warming her. "We have to put our trust in Him, Katy" he softly repeated back to her.

Later, sometime in the night, Kate's eyes popped open. *He called me Katy.* She turned on her side, snuggled down with a smile on her lips, and closed her eyes.

Chapter 4

Max was up at daybreak, determined to get the wagon in working order by end of day. The likelihood of building it back to the original was slim to none, especially with limited tools. He figured the best option was to revamp it into a two-wheel cart and leave some of their belongings behind.

Now where'd that blame hammer run off to? "Boys? You see my hammer?"

"Nope."

Max was getting irritated. "Kate, you seen the hammer anywhere?" She hadn't noticed it either but organized a search, sending Josh and Joey off in different directions while she headed for the cave.

Max walked in circles around their camp, kicking burned logs from the previous night's fire as if someone had mistaken his hammer for a piece of firewood. *How in heaven's name could a hammer just up and disappear?*

The entire morning was lost, and still no hammer. Kate fixed a noontime meal of fried potatoes and onions, and after she quietly gave thanks to the Lord, she offered to read a passage from the Bible. Though no hammer was to be found, she had come out of the cave with Mrs. Reed's Bible.

The boys were captivated by her reading and, truth be told, so was Max. His eyes strayed to her lips, and her voice was sweet like music. He thought, *it feels like we are family.* The hammer was forgotten, at least momentarily. Max stood after a bit needing to get to work, with or without the hammer.

Kate interrupted his thoughts. "Perhaps we should pick some berries this afternoon. What do you boys think about another cobbler for supper?" With wide matching grins, they agreed wholeheartedly and then suddenly looked at each other. Their smiles faded into an apprehensive look, like a serious dilemma had occurred to them simultaneously.

Max almost didn't catch it. He studied his young brothers, narrowing his eyes. "Is there a problem helping Miss Kate pick berries?"

"No, no. No problem." The boys looked at each other, guilt written all over their faces.

Max faced them fully. "Well then, let's *all* go pick berries. Right now would be good."

———

They followed a path along the river, single file: Josh, Joe, Kate, and Max. When they rounded the bend where the berry brambles grew, Josh stopped dead in his tracks. Joey, Kate, and Max abruptly collided into each other. Seven Indians were standing there like statues, their horses in tow. Three braves stood on each side, wearing a single feather in their headbands. The one in the middle, seemed to have superior status, his headdress sporting three feathers. His arms were crossed, and the look in his eyes was menacing. He mumbled native words.

Max instinctively stepped in front of his "family," his arms drawing them behind him, so that the twins were peeking out from under his right arm and Kate under his left. "We're simply peaceful berry pickers; we mean no harm. No harm at all," Max implored.

"We bring peace. Peace." He placed a hand on his heart for emphasis, but he wasn't making much headway with the seven Indians.

The boys were part scared to death and part intrigued, having learned some about Indian customs and heard talk of Indian attacks. Kate was terrified—that is, until she spotted it. "What in heaven's name?" She whirled past Max and marched, arms swinging and skirt swaying, right up to the chief, or whoever he was. "That belongs to me!" She grabbed the silver locket, yanking its chain hard against his neck. "Where'd you get this? It was my mother's. I cut my teeth on this locket. Give it back this instant!"

The Indian towered over Kate, scowling. He reached behind his neck and unlatched the chain, then gingerly dangled it in front of her nose.

At that moment, Joey darted to her side and grabbed her skirt, feeling protective. "Thsee thsed, give it back."

Max, horrified, ran to their side, Josh in his grip. *Oh Lord, she's gonna get us all scalped.*

Kate was able to grasp the locket and open it. "See?" She turned the faded image toward the chief. "This is my mother." All six other Indians moved in for a closer look, and then their leader, with a hint of fear in his eyes, mumbled something and dropped it into her hand.

"He wants to make a trade," Josh said evenly. Max thought it preposterous that a nine-year-old would know anything about an Indian wanting to make a trade.

"Trade," said Chief Three Feathers. Hastily Max surveyed their immediate possessions, which included two empty buckets.

Kate suggested in a hushed tone, "Maybe something back at camp?"

The big Indian said, "Trade. Camp."

Oh great. We're doomed, Max thought. "Yes, all right, wait right here, and we'll bring back a good trade. From camp." He grabbed Kate's hand, instructed the boys to hold each other's hands, and led the way back down the path, making sure all four of them stuck together. The seven Indians jumped on their horses and followed behind in single file. *Wonderful. They're going with us. They'll probably burn us at the stake.*

The Indians dismounted and surveyed their campsite. Max knew they had nothing to trade, not a thing of value. He saw plainly how pathetic they really were. All they had were broken crates, rusty pots and pans, ragged bedrolls, and a battered wagon, broken in half. After a quick survey, the chief walked his moccasin-covered feet slowly toward where Sampson and Delilah were tied to a tree. He ran a hand down each back, checked their teeth and their feet, and declared, "Trade," as he patted Delilah on the rump.

"Not Delilah!" the boys shouted in unison.

"Take Sampson," begged Josh. "He's better! Delilah, she's stubborn and ornery. We'll trade Sampson,"

"Yeah," cried Joey. "Take Thampthon!"

The big Indian glanced at the boys and turned back to Delilah. He stroked her flank and once again made his declaration. "Trade."

Max was scrambling for something—anything—enticing that might distract from Delilah. The boys loved the old mule; she was a pet to them. It was bad enough that they'd had to give up Johnny Boy, their shabby old stray dog. Delilah was sweet and cooperative, and she seemed to recognize Josh and Joe when they were around her. She even nibbled at their thick blond hair, bringing fits of laughter.

Kate looked at Max and then the boys. "Here." She faced Three Feathers, holding out the locket. "Take this. Delilah is not for trade."

Max shook his head. *She's a plucky little thing. Brave.* "No, Kate. You keep the locket. It belonged to your ma; it means something. You can't put a price on it. Delilah—well, she's been a good mule, but nothing compared to your ma's locket."

Josh and Joey looked at the ground, trying to be brave.

———

That night, under a starlit sky, Max tucked the boys in. He tried to lift their spirits by retelling stories of Oregon, hoping they would look forward once again to that land of milk and honey. Josh asked Max to pray.

"About our new home in Oregon?" Max asked.

"No, Max. About Delilah. Ask God to please take care of her."

"And Maxth," Joe added, "ya better say one for me and Josh too. We, uh, kind of, uh—hid the hammer."

Kate was sitting on the opposite side of the fire, swallowing back tears as she heard Max praying for the little gray mule those boys loved. They had endured so much loss in their young lives. *Oh Lord, why is everything so hard? It goes from bad to worse. My heart is aching for these children. And aching still for my dear father. Will I ever see him again?*

Max came to her side, offering a cup of hot coffee. "Here, ma'am, drink this stuff. It'll do ya a world of good."

She smiled up at him and took the cup, her eyes never leaving his. She knew he was a good man, protector of his family, hardworking, responsible, and notably handsome. His hair, blond like the boys', was in bad need of a trim, but she had noticed he took a bar of soap and a shaving blade to his jaw in the mornings. And the few times he'd laughed, she'd become aware of a dimple in his right cheek. Like right then. He was smiling at her—a big smile, his straight teeth white in the firelight.

He sat down next to her and was quiet for a while. They stared into the fire, both in deep thought. Then he said, "Why in heaven's name would they hide the hammer?"

"Hmmm," Kate mused. "Perhaps they didn't want you to fix the wagon."

Sure enough, Joshua and Joseph eventually confessed to Kate's speculation that they did in fact hide the hammer, burying it in the berry vines, to stall leaving. What they didn't come clean about was the *reason*. They made some feeble explanation about their fine campsite and Kate's cooking, especially the berry cobbler. But the truth was, in their way of thinking, if they stayed long enough, Max might decide to marry Kate.

Chapter 5

At long last, Max got back to work on the wagon, after the hammer episode, the Indian trouble, Kate's locket trauma, and the Delilah ordeal. He figured it would take a good day's work to get the wagon in hauling condition and probably another to determine what would go and what would stay, and then to get packed up to head west. Although it would be a bit of a risk with the weather, he was sure once they got Kate delivered to the next town and safely on the stagecoach heading east, he and the boys could make up for lost time.

But the excitement he expected to feel was swapped with an ache somewhere in his belly. It didn't feel right—him going west and Kate going east. She was so affectionate and caring of the boys. She also was a good cook, a hard worker, and never complained. And she was beautiful, inside and out. He admired the way her skirt fit snug around her tiny waist; curves in all the right places. Max realized he was watching her with his mouth open and quickly recovered, turning his attention to the job at hand.

Josh and Joey helped their big brother as best they could. But after the noon meal, Kate walked with them to the river then handed over a bar of soap and a set of instructions. She left a bundle of clean clothes, the only ones besides those on their back, on a big rock. They were to leave their grimy clothes in the washtub she had hauled to the riverbank, not only to wash their clothes but everything she could get her hands on. She knew there would be no room to haul the tub when they broke camp and headed out the day after next.

That thought left her with an ache. She had to get back to her father, no matter what. But she was already feeling hollowness inside for Josh and Joey. She had grown to love those two. And Max? She couldn't really explain the way she felt about Max. He made her feel safe; he made her feel appreciated. She even felt pretty, especially after seeing him looking at her. She fanned her face, suddenly warm. *What's come over you, Kate? Get back to the washtub.*

Everyone was quiet after supper that night, not wanting to bring up the next day. They had packed up the barest of essentials into their now two-wheeled cart, ready to be hitched to their one remaining mule, Sampson—the one with an independent attitude, to say the least. Josh and Joey would take turns driving the cart, since they were light. The one not driving would ride double with Kate on their horse, Moses. Max would ride Solomon, his tall buckskin.

Kate tucked the boys in their bedrolls and was praying silently when Max knelt beside her. "Them young'uns are gonna miss you real bad, Kate. You've been so kind to them. I thank ya for that." Kate kept her head down; she nodded but was unable to speak. They sat in silence for a while, and then she stood abruptly and turned toward her own bedroll. "We best get some rest, Max."

Kate was bone tired, but sleep wouldn't come. She tossed and turned, trying to pray, giving her troubles to the Lord one minute, taking them back the next. She lay there gazing at the stars, reflecting on the past few days. It seemed like an eternity ago since she'd seen her father; since deciding to take him to Oregon had seemed so right.

Just then one of the boys cried out, and she thought he was having a dream. But she realized it was more like moaning. She slipped over to them and gently felt both heads. One of them was feverish; she wasn't sure if it was Joe or Josh. Quietly she moved to the pail of fresh water, carried it near the boy's bedroll, and tore off a section of her petticoat. Tenderly she placed the cool rag on the feverish forehead and stroked his mop of golden hair. His eyes fluttered but closed again in sleep. Once more he moaned, and then coughed—a deep, croupy cough. She was pretty sure it was Joe and that he was a very sick boy.

Throughout the night, Kate kept cool cloths on Joe's brow, but the fever became worse, the cough more frequent. Suddenly he struggled, trying to get out from under the heavy quilt, but he was too weak. His big eyes looked up to hers. "I'm gonna be thick, ma'am." Before morning light, Josh followed suit with a fever, moaning, coughing, and retching.

Max was awakened by singing. He wondered if he'd died and gone to heaven. It sounded like the voice of an angel singing ever so sweetly. Kate was wrapped in his mother's quilt, kneeling over the boys, softly singing a hymn. He noticed the cloths on their foreheads. *Are they sick? And I slept through it?* He got up, stiff as a board from the hard ground, and stumbled to their side. "What's wrong, boys? Are you sick?"

"Oh, Max, I'm so worried about them. Joey started first, then Josh. They're burnin' up with fever. Do you have any medicine in your supplies? Anything that might bring the fever down?"

Max said he didn't and then fetched tin cups. "Maybe we can get some water down them." The boys were parched and so weak and limp with fever they could barely sip from the cups offered them.

As dawn broke, Max got the fire revived by tossing on the remaining scraps from their broken wagon. Kate had stayed awake all night; he could tell by dark circles under her eyes. "I'll sit with the boys, Kate. Try to get some rest. Pretty sure we won't be travelin' today."

Kate slowly stood, gathered herself after sitting so long, and walked to the fire, her back to him, the quilt still wrapped around her. "I'll make some coffee." It was barely a whisper; she was so wrought with worry. The boys were sleeping soundly, but still burning with fever, beads of sweat on their brows.

Max bowed his head, closed his eyes, and prayed, "Lord, please bring healing to Josh and Joe. It doesn't matter when or even if we ever get it to Oregon. Just make them well. Please, God. Make my little brothers well." He looked up at the sound of Kate pouring coffee, and his jaw dropped. She had set aside the quilt and was wearing a faded blue work shirt and *britches*. Once they'd been his, then patched and washed and stored away for the boys. They were still too big for them and now too small for him. But on Kate they fit perfectly. In fact, he quite admired the way she looked in those britches.

Kate turned toward him, then blushed a bit because of the way he stared at her. She handed him a cup of coffee, saying, "I had to bury it. My dress. Joey, well, and Josh too—well, uh—I had to bury it."

———

Max and Kate fashioned a canopy with the tarp Max had been sleeping on, to shade the boys from the bright September sun. Other than coughing spells and trying to take small sips of water, they slept all day, pale and limp like two rag dolls. Max tried to keep busy, rearranging the cart, pounding in a few more nails, checking the horses' feet a dozen times as the day dragged on. Kate could not leave her patients; she continued to nurse and pray for them, but their fevers lingered.

Toward evening, Kate unconsciously prepared a small meal for Max but ate very little herself, only because he insisted. Again that night she, with Max by her side, kept vigil over the boys, cooling their brows; singing to them and praying over them while they slept. Before the first light of dawn, Max stretched out next to the boys and fell asleep too.

Kate was weary, resting her head on her knees, desperately clinging to her faith that the Lord would restore Josh and Joe, that the fever would soon break. She lifted her head, sensing a "presence," someone nearby. As she looked over her shoulder, and close to the wall of rock, she spotted a woman. In the light of dawn. She could barely see that it was a young Indian woman, a papoose on her back. She stood straight and very still. Kate cautiously stood and faced her, her eyes darting above and beyond to make sure she was alone, and then slowly walked toward her.

"Peace," the young Indian said quietly as she placed one hand over her heart and held out a leather pouch with her other.

"Peace," replied Kate, placing her shaky hand over her own heart. With mostly gestures and few words, the young Indian woman conveyed she had brought medicine for the sickness. She demonstrated with graceful hand movements how to mix a few pinches of the dried leaves into hot water for the boys to drink. All the while, her baby slept tranquilly, used to the bending and moving of his mother. Kate accepted the pouch, believing it was not by chance this woman appeared from nowhere, but was an answer to prayer.

As the Indian woman turned to slip back to wherever she came from, she looked over her shoulder and smiled at Kate. "The mule, Delilah – good."

———

Had it not been for the pouch of herbs, Max would have thought Kate was hallucinating about the Indian woman appearing out of nowhere, somehow knowing sickness inhabited their camp. An hour or more had passed since Max and Kate administered the medicine when a gravelly little voice came from the sickbed. "Any cobbler left?" Josh had pulled up on his elbows.

Kate went to him and drew him into a vigorous hug. "Oh, Josh! Sweetheart. You're gonna be all right." At the commotion, Joey stirred. "Did thumbody sthay cobbler?"

Kate laughed and cried at the same time as she scooped Joey into the hug. "Oh my boys. Praise God! You're all right."

Max hovered over them, chuckling and shaking his head. Then he hastily stood and turned his back to them. Kate looked up to see he had removed his hat and was looking heavenward. *Thank you, Lord Jesus, thank you,* Max silently prayed. A tear or two escaped his eyes as well.

Kate slipped quietly up behind him. "Max?" He turned to her, and their eyes locked in silent relief. He pulled her into his arms. She didn't resist but held him close, knowing they had a shared understanding. Kate could not exactly define the emotion she was feeling in that moment: gratitude, joy, maybe even love?

Josh and Joey rested much of the day, still pale enough Kate could count the identical freckles on their identical noses, but enjoying every bite of Kate's berry syrup drizzled over biscuits. She had prepared and packed the delicious treat for travel, but she didn't hesitate to unpack it for the nourishment of *her* boys.

As the day wore on, the boys gained strength and were chattering like their old selves by evening. Finally, they would leave in the morning, as long as Josh and Joe were strong enough for the journey.

The night air was definitely cooler. Max and Kate sat by the fire with their usual tin cups of coffee, chatting—well, mostly Kate was chatting—about the incredible events of the past few days. Then she began to giggle and finally threw her head back into a full-on laugh.

"What?" Max looked puzzled but couldn't help smiling at her uncontrollable laughter. Every time she tried to collect herself, she started shaking with the giggles again. "Kate, what's so blame funny? Here, drink some coffee." He filled her cup, thinking it would calm her down, but instead she spewed it straight into the fire, which made her laugh even more.

Finally, in fragments of sentence, she got out, "I can't believe," clamping her hand over her mouth, "I can't believe," now bending in half, "that, that you—that you caught me!" And she continued to laugh until tears ran down her cheeks.

Max turned to face her, then wiped away the tears on her face with his thumb. "Kate." He paused. "Katy, when we leave here in the morning?"

She looked into his big brown eyes, sobering. "Yes, Max?"

"I'm taking you to your father."

Chapter 6

They were a sight, Joey driving the cart, trying to keep moving with stubborn old Sampson; Josh and Kate riding double on Moses; Max riding Solomon. Their bedrolls were tied behind the saddles, and pots and pans and other oddities were all tied to the cart. Sampson determined the pace, which was mostly slow. Unless the trail narrowed, they rode four abreast, conversing, laughing, and relaxed. *Just like one big happy family*, Max thought.

Kate broke into his thinking. "Since everyone in your family seems to have a Bible name, including the animals, where would one find Max in the Bible?"

All three brothers laughed out loud. "His name is Jeremiah Maxwell," declared Josh. "Pa named ever livin' thing in our family with a Bible name, and us boys got the middle name of some ol' ancestor."

"Well, that satisfies my curiosity, except for one thing. Didn't I hear you once had a dog named Johnny Boy?"

Max chuckled, the dimple in his cheek pronounced. *So appealing*, Kate thought, *downright cute*. He replied, "Johnny Boy showed up on the back porch one day, lookin' like he been livin' in the desert— all scraggly, obviously a stray. Pa said the boys could keep him, so long as they took care of him and gave him a good ol' Bible name."

It was Joey's turn. "So, we named him John the Baptist."

Kate burst out laughing at the thought: a dog named John the Baptist. And then she realized something. Joey's speech. It was perfect.

"By the way, Kate," Max said. "I have something to ask *you*. Who is Silas?"

———

Silas knew she was praying for him. Otherwise, his scalp would be on display right next to Boss's. Once they had hauled the loot from the stolen coach into a deep cave off the beaten path, Boss had ordered Silas to get rid of it and then turn all but two horses loose. "How in the world I s'posed to hide that blame thang? All painted red with gold curlicues?"

He drove it for half a day before coming to the summit on the trail where passengers liked to stop and marvel at the view; like being on top of the world. It was a good thirty paces to the edge, and Silas thought if he could get close enough, he would then just push the coach over. He unhitched the horses, except for two, while he was a safe distance from the drop-off, and then coaxed them in a slow walk as close as he dared. *Good Lord, please keep me from stumblin'—in more ways than one.* This reminded him that it was a good thing he'd given up the moonshine.

Cautiously Silas unhitched the two horses and led them to a tree, where he tied them securely. It took all his strength and several heaves before the big red coach leaned, a front wheel slipped over the edge, the coach teetered, and then it crashed into a mass of red and gold splinters on the valley floor far below.

It was just a matter of time before Silas would figure out a different way, now that he had come back to the Lord. He was sure God had a plan for him far better than the outlaw life. Like Kate had said, he didn't have to live like that anymore. *I'm done bein' an outlaw. I'm gonna tell Boss as soon as I deliver these here horses.*

Silas got on one of the horses and rode hard—into a new life. But he was too late. Indians had gotten there first. The hideout had been ransacked, their loot was scattered from one end to the other, and Boss was lying sprawled in the middle of it all, as dead as a doornail. A chill came over Silas, running down his spine; his big calloused hands began to shake. *I best skedaddle. Pronto.*

But then he noticed a heap of pretty colors, lady's frocks, and other lacey things. He knew it had to be Kate's, since there had been no other women on the stage. That was the reason they had taken her hostage; she was the only woman. Silas righted the trunk and quickly stuffed everything he could into it, then dragged it deeper into the cave, not sure how he would retrieve it. But he owed her that at the very least. The little woman had changed his life.

———

It was early afternoon on their third day of traveling when Max, Kate, and the boys got their first glimpse of the Wells Fargo stage stop, a dot on the horizon. Kate's heart skipped a beat with anticipation. She would soon be in the warm embrace of her father.

It had been her turn to drive the cart, and after a few hours, she was ready to slaughter Sampson. Even though she had encouraged the boys to be patient with the stubborn animal, her own patience was at its limit. She couldn't get to her father fast enough, and Sampson had the audacity not only stop in his tracks, but also sit. The three Reed brothers, straddling their horses, were entertained by the whole thing.

The boys were trying to get Sampson to move, yelling, "Eeeehah! Git! Git! Yah! Giddup! Yip! Yip! Yip!" when something in the distance caught their eye: a cloud of dust way off between the stage stop and them. It was more than tumbleweed. Kate thought it might be an animal. The closer it got, the more it appeared to hobble. It was coming closer and closer as fast as it could muster.

Suddenly Josh and Joey flew off their horse, plummeting to the ground. They scrambled to their feet in a full run toward the limping animal until boys and dog where one: the boys laughing, the dog barking, all of them stirring up dust like a Kansas cyclone.

Max shook his head. "Will wonders never cease. It's Johnny Boy."

———

The inn looked nearly deserted except for one old cowboy sitting on the porch, idling the time away. Johnny Boy hobbled up the steps and went directly to him and rested his chin on the old man's knee. "Well, ain't you somethin'," the man chuckled as he patted the dog's head like no one else was around.

Max, right behind Johnny Boy, called out a friendly hello. The old man evidently didn't hear well; his focus remained on the dog. Kate, a few paces behind Max, stopped dead in her tracks. The old cowboy was her father.

"Papa?" He didn't look up, captivated with the dog.

Just then Millie burst through the door with her usual exuberance, expecting to call Clayton for supper. "Kate!" She clamped her hand over her mouth then gathered the younger woman in a hearty embrace. "Oh my, we've been worried to death about you. Didn't know if we'd ever see you again." She clutched her chest and choked back tears.

Kate was a little overwhelmed by the whole scene, and her father didn't seem to notice any of them. He didn't seem to see her or hear the commotion. He just patted Johnny Boy. The twins approached the old cowboy, and he vacantly looked their way.

Millie said, "Why don't we all go in to supper. You can go right through to the back porch and wash up." She looked at Kate with sadness. "It'll take a little time, honey. Be patient. He'll know ya again." And then she said to him, "Come along, Clayton. Time to eat." He slowly got up from the rocking chair and took Millie's arm, and they headed inside.

Millie had one of her helpers guide Clayton to his room for a nap. Kate was mystified, confused. Of course she was grateful her father seemed well and content, that people were caring for him. But she had barely been gone two weeks, and he didn't recognize her. Would he ever know her again?

Josh and Joe ate Millie's hearty meal with gusto, mopping up every last drop of gravy with thick slices of bread. Max too seemed revived after supper, but Kate picked at her food, too troubled to eat. She felt a bit better after soaking in a hot bath, which was a long time in coming. Millie set out a fresh uniform for her, a dark-blue cotton dress with a high-button collar and crisp white apron. "It's all I have to offer, honey, but it's clean and looks mighty good on ya. Besides, I could use a little extra help in the dinin' room."

Kate suddenly felt very grateful for the care given her father. "Thank you for your kindness, Millie. I am happy to help in any way I can. Max and the boys too. They're good hands, hard workers, and—well—we really don't have any place to go now, until spring."

Millie laughed and regarded Kate warmly. "Well, bless the Lord. I'm comin' up short-handed this fall, inside and out. If y'all are willin' and able, I got plenty of work."

Millie took to Josh and Joey right away, and the feeling was mutual. She never could tell who was who, but she called them "twinners" and loved to squish their cheeks until their lips puckered and to scruff up their hair. In the evenings after supper, the boys brought in firewood and collected a little basket left strictly for Millie's twinners: an extra helping of pie or sticky buns or sugar cookies.

Millie considered Max an answer to prayer, since Henry Weaver, who had run the livery for years, was old and stooped with back troubles. The old black man was full of fascinating tales from his days as a slave in the South. He had a unique way with horses too; he was able to somehow persuade the most cantankerous beasts to obey.

"Mr. Henry?" Joey asked. "Think you could make Sampson mind us better?"

"Oh ma Lawdy." Henry scratched his ear and shook his head, laughing. "I ain't no miracle man. Lawdy, Lawdy." He slapped his thigh, and his eyes twinkled in spite of the haze beginning to obscure his vision.

Max had always been good with horses and at a young age had learned the art of making horseshoes and fitting them properly. But Henry was teaching him new ways of breaking and training young horses.

After a week at Millie's Inn, the name the boys chose for it, Max and his little family had developed a rhythm: Kate working in the dining room and sleeping in a guest room, Max and the boys caring for the animals, chopping wood, and keeping the fires tended. They had a section to themselves in the bunkhouse with a stove, three cots, and thick quilts. Stagecoach travel had slowed a bit because of weather, but Millie ran the place like a full house, keeping her staff well taken care of in exchange for the work they did.

Chapter 7

Every evening after supper, Clayton, with Johnny Boy at his side, sat in a rocker in front of the stone fireplace, gazing absently into the fire. When her duties were completed one night, Kate sat down in the chair next to his and sipped her coffee. No words were spoken between them. The only sound was the creaking of his rocking chair. After a bit, Josh and Joey came in to check the firewood, and Kate invited them to pull up a chair too.

When Max showed up, holding a cup of coffee, her heart beat a little faster. And he rearranged the boys so he could sit next to her. "Just like old times," he said softly. Then he winked and smiled. Kate loved his dimple. Except for the fact that her father didn't recognize her, she felt content, sitting warm by the fire with those she cared about. The custom that had started back at their campsite, became a nightly ritual.

After Millie helped Clayton to his room one evening, Max sent the boys off to the bunkhouse and stayed behind with Kate. They sat quietly just watching the fire. "I've been prayin' each night he would know ya, Kate," Max said. "That come mornin', when you pour his coffee, he shows a bit of recognition or just says your name."

Kate looked at him, her eyes big in the firelight, though sad. "Oh, Max, it breaks my heart. I fear he will never know me again."

He touched her cheek, tucked a loose strand of hair behind her ear, and said, "Sometimes what helps me is to think about the things that could've happened, but didn't. When I thank God for what *didn't* happen, I begin to see more clearly the good things that did. A lot has happened in both our lives, Kate, but Scripture says that all things work together for good to those who love the Lord. All things, Katy."

———

One afternoon, Millie asked Kate if she would mind moving to another chamber because they would need every guest room that night. Kate said with a grin, "I would feel privileged to sleep in the broom closet." They went to her room to gather her meager belongings, then Kate followed Millie down the long hallway until they came to a door at the end.

When Millie turned the key and opened the door, Kate was stunned. Slowly she followed Millie into the enchanting room. The focal point was a big carved wooden bed, a feather bed no less, covered with a cloud of a comforter and piled with fluffy pillows— all white. The lace curtains were white too, as was a scarf on the bedside table. A small stove crackled with warmth in the corner; a rocking chair was nearby, and a writing desk in front of a tall window was arranged with paper, a feather pen, a Bible, and a lamp.

Next to the window hung a faded image of a young man and woman. Kate thought they were a very handsome couple. The woman held a bouquet of wildflowers, and she knew it was Millie, many years before. On the opposite wall, next to the door, was an exquisite antique wardrobe and, next to that, a bowl and pitcher with sweet-smelling soap and a white towel draped over the edge. Delicately embroidered on the towel in faintest pink was the letter G.

"Millie!" Kate exclaimed almost breathlessly. "This room is beautiful! So charming. It must be reserved for someone exceptionally special."

"That it is, honey. That it is. Go ahead and sit on the bed, Kate. I have a story to tell you." Millie sat in the rocker by the fire. Smiling over at Kate, she took a deep breath and began.

———

It had been over twenty years since Millie married the man of her dreams. Dallas Thatcher was handsome, a hard-working cowboy who had fallen for Millie instantly. Like so many other young couples, they dreamed of heading west and staking a claim in Oregon. By the time they had sold their land in Oklahoma and saved enough money to join a wagon train, God had blessed them with a beautiful baby girl. Grace was seven months old when they were finally ready to head west. Like her mother, she had the bluest eyes and a head of feathery pale-blond hair. Her cheeks were rosy, and so was her disposition. Gracie K, as her father called her, was their pride and joy.

They planned, purchased, and packed for a month of Sundays, excitedly preparing for the journey. All manner of provisions—beans and potatoes, flour, sugar, cornmeal, a crate of chickens, pots and pans, bedding and clothing, and everything they owned—was packed in their covered wagon. Dallas had built a bed for Grace, a sturdy compartment that Millie lined with thick padding. It was like a white cloud to lay her in, safely tucked just behind the wagon seat. Heavy flour sacks kept the little bed stabilized, and Grace slept peacefully as the wagon rumbled along, pulled by the Thatcher oxen.

Grace was a remarkable child, uniquely pretty and always content. In the evenings, as families circled up for the night, Grace was often the center of attention. Youngsters of every age begged to hold her and giggled every time she made a move or wrinkled her nose.

With the exception of an occasional breakdown and a brief summer storm, the wagon train was on schedule, making slow but steady progress. Soldiers from Ft. Laramie had accompanied them through Indian Territory without incident. Perhaps it gave the pioneers a false sense of security; perhaps they let their guard down.

It happened so fast. From out of nowhere, a band of Indians attacked, screaming war cries, killing without mercy. Dallas grabbed his rifle and started shooting, yelling at Millie to get back with the baby. Frantically she scrambled to get to Grace, but something hard hit the back of her head, knocking her out.

When she came to, sometime later, in a daze, she looked over to see Dallas lying next to her, an arrow in his chest. To her horror, he was gone—killed by Indians, just like that. His face looked peaceful. There was no blood on his shirt, so she knew his death must have happened in an instant.

Around their wagon was evidence that no one but she had survived the attack. Dread filled her as she pulled back the heavy canvas behind the wagon seat, praying her daughter was safe, though not a whimper had come from her bed. Nothing had been disturbed, their belongings were still packed tightly, the flour sacks that surrounded Gracie's bed stood like a sentinels. But Gracie was gone. The bed her father had made, the puffy lining—all gone.

———

By then, Millie was sitting on the bed next to Kate, both women weeping. "I searched for my Gracie for days—days that turned into years. She was gone without a trace. At least I know Dallas is in heaven with the Lord, but I don't know if my girl is dead or alive, if someone has cared for her or mistreated her. I'm trustin' the Lord though, and believin' that I'll see her again. That's why I moved here and took on runnin' this place, where travelers are comin' from every direction. Maybe I'll hear something, see someone that knows her. I've built up a fine establishment, but that's not my reason for being here. And this room? It's just waiting for the day she comes home."

Kate wrapped her arms around Millie. "Oh, Millie, I am truly sorry. You are so kind and gracious to everyone who comes through the door. You have a servant's heart, lifting everyone else's spirits. You reflect the love of Jesus more than anyone I've ever met. I would never have known that underneath your lovely countenance is a broken heart." Kate could not imagine the pain Millie bore. "I will pray for Grace—for Gracie K," she promised, smiling through tears. "How old would she be?"

Millie blew her nose and smiled. "Nineteen—tomorrow. Oh, and the K. The K is for Katherine. Grace Katherine."

———

That night Kate sat in the rocker of that lovely room: Grace Thatcher's room. She felt unworthy to be there but somehow knew it brought a bit of comfort to Millie. She stared at Dallas and Millie's wedding picture; they were young, full of hope. Then she thought of Max. He had been so caring and sweet as they sat by the fire the night before. She rested her head on the chair back and began to think about the things that *didn't* happen, like Max said.

Just in the past few weeks, she could have taken a bullet to the head, but she didn't. She could still be held captive, but she wasn't. Like the prodigal son, her captor had come back to the Lord and helped her escape. She could have broken her neck when Silas booted her out of the coach, but she didn't. And when she slipped and fell off the cliff, she could have been killed. But she wasn't. Instead someone caught her. A wonderful someone. Kate smiled at the thought. And the boys. They could have died with fever, but they didn't. And her father, she might have never seen him again. But she was with him now . He was alive and being cared for. In fact, he seemed to be physically stronger, not so pale and almost dignified, the way he once was, dressed in Dallas Thatcher's cowboy garb, hat, and boots, which all fit him to a tee.

Oh Lord, I've been so blind. All I ever do is ask
for things, beg for help. Tonight, Lord, I just want

to thank You. Thank You for everything that didn't happen. Thank You that You've been with me just as You promised. And Jesus? Please, please, Lord, bring Gracie K home.

Kate looked over at the featherbed, so soft, inviting. *And one more thing: I could still be sleeping on that hard, cold, lumpy ground. But I'm not.*

Chapter 8

The next morning, Kate was up extra early, face scrubbed shiny, hair pulled up in a neat bun, ready for the day. She felt a kind of peaceful excitement. She tied on a clean white apron, said her good mornings to the kitchen help, and began her day serving guests in the dining room. She had fresh energy in her step as she greeted each table and poured hot coffee.

Clayton shuffled in an hour or so after the bulk of guests had finished breakfast. He slowly sat at the first table he came to, as was his habit, and Kate strode over to pour his coffee with a cheerful, "Good morning, sir." He didn't look up. She added cream to cool the hot liquid and a spoon of sugar the way he liked it. "Looks to be some storm clouds rollin' in this mornin'," she said, speaking as she had to earlier diners. Her father had no response. "Enjoy your coffee, sir, and I will bring you a sweet roll right away."

She turned and was heading back toward the kitchen doors when she heard, "Thank you, Katy darlin'." His voice was gravely, but unmistakable.

She stopped abruptly, splashing coffee on her white apron, and whirled around to face him. "Papa?" Just as quickly as he had spoken, his gaze turned back to staring at his coffee. The empty look had returned. *But he did remember! For a few seconds he knew me. He said, "Katy, Katy darlin'." I must tell Max.*

She flew into the kitchen, plunked the pot on the stove, and ran out the back, across the yard to the barn where Max was mucking stalls. "Max! Max!" He tossed the pitchfork and hurried to her. "He called me Katy! He recognized me, Max, just for a moment, but he knew it was me. Papa recognized me."

Max scooped her into a strong hug, lifting her feet off the ground and whirling her in a circle. "Thank you, Lord. I knew he would, Kate. Just didn't know when."

Kate said, "Last night I thought of all the things that didn't happen, just like you said Max. I gave thanks, one thing at a time, and it was like a heavy weight lifted. I could have been killed—three times. But I wasn't. I could have been lost to Papa forever, but I wasn't, and the boys—they could've died, Max. But they didn't." They remained in each other's arms as she excitedly rattled off her list of things that didn't happen.

From somewhere behind Max came matching voices, "Hallelujah!" Two sets of big brown eyes peeked around the next stall. The boys hurried to Kate as she knelt in the straw in her white apron. She gathered them into her arms, doing that thing again, where she laughed and cried at the same time. "Josh! Joey! Oh my goodness. I love you boys." She squeezed them tight then looked up at Max. Their eyes remained on each other, and to herself she said, *I love you too, Max.*

As they gathered in front of the fire with Millie, Clayton, and of course, Johnny Boy, Kate picked up the Bible. She hadn't felt like reading Scripture or singing since they'd arrived back at Millie's. That night, whether or not her father recognized her, she was going to read his favorite passage, the Twenty-Third Psalm. That morning he had known her, and that's all that mattered..

Everyone was charmed by her reading and even more so when she led them in a hymn. Clayton rocked his chair and tapped his foot to the music, the trace of a smile on his face. After Max prayed, everyone said their amens.

When they looked up, there stood old Henry with his fiddle. "Ah's hearin' some fine music comin' out back." With that, he pulled his violin to his shoulder and started in to play. Clayton brightened a bit. Then the swinging doors from the kitchen swung open, and there stood Tom Carter, the head cook, with his mouth harp. Millie made a declaration to herself and scurried to the storage room to drag out a gutbucket.

The little band played a lively version of "What a Friend We Have in Jesus," and everyone sang along, clapping cheerfully. The noise drew a few guests downstairs to see what it was all about. Before long, Henry got going on "Cotton Eyed Joe," and Millie instructed the twinners to roll up the rugs, push the tables back, and arrange the chairs to face the dance floor. Smiles brightened the boys' faces, as they grew excited over the whole thing.

"May I have this dance, Miss Kate?" Max asked. She blushed and had started to decline when he whipped her up and out onto the dance floor. Both surprised each other that they knew how to dance—at least barn-dance style. Kate could not stop smiling as Max twirled her around the floor, catching her and pulling her to him. Soon she was laughing, no longer intimidated by the crowd cheering them on.

Out of the corner of his eye, Max noticed the boys talking with their heads together. They were definitely up to something. Another couple, guests that had come downstairs, joined them on the dance floor, and Henry jumped right into another lively number. Tom kept right up with his mouth harp, and Millie plunked away on the gutbucket.

Out of nowhere, Max felt a tug on his pant leg and slowed to see Joey. "I'm a cuttin' in, Max."

Whatever happened to shy little Joey? Max thought. "Well, hold on there—

Kate interrupted. "Oh, excuse me, Mr. Reed, but according to my dance card, this dance is for a Mr. Reed. Joseph Reed." Joe lit up and moved right in between Kate and Max, and got ahold of her, just the way Max had. Kate did the leading, but right there, before God and everybody, Joey was dancing. *Dancing with his girl!* he thought. The next thing Max knew, the plunking ceased, and Josh was dancing with Millie. Max was relegated to the gutbucket while his little brothers were having the time of their life, dancing the night away.

Before everyone called it a night, Millie and Kate brought out a big tin of sugar cookies and a two jugs of cool apple cider for refreshments. It was indeed a real party: dancing and laughter, music and sugar cookies. Not all that long ago Kate hadn't known any of those folks—such an unlikely blend of people, each with an untold story. Yet there they were together, in common fellowship, enjoying each other. She couldn't help but hug each one as they headed to their rooms, with Millie helping Clayton, until just she and Max remained.

They had offered to put the tables and chairs back in order and roll out the rugs. Kate was bustling about moving chairs when Max slipped up and took her hand. "One more dance?" Before she could object and point out that there was no music, he led her out to the dance floor. "After all, I barely had a chance after you-know-who and you-know-who cut in the whole blame evenin'."

Kate laughed. "One more dance." He drew her close, dancing slowly. This was not the Cotton Eyed Joe kind of dance, but her heart was beating like it. His hand at the small of her back pulled her closer. Her silky hair brushed his cheek. They danced without music, both mesmerized in the moment. "Kate," he whispered in her ear. "Katy." He could hardly breathe. He quit moving and looked down at her face, beautiful in the lamplight's glow. They studied each other's eyes, each other's lips. Then, with great tenderness, Max moved his lips to hers and kissed her. Kate kissed back. It was the first kiss for both. Before the dance ended, they kissed again, this time with deep passion.

Thunder, Silas's faithful dappled gray, plodded on courageously in the face of a blizzard like Silas had never seen. He was cold in spite of the buffalo hide draped over his back, bone tired, and starving to death. *Lord, I'm beginnin' ta think yer not out there, that ya don't care nothin' about me. Maybe I shoulda stayed in that last town. But I knew I'd be tempted if I did. I'm tryin' to do right, Lord. It jest ain't gettin' me nowhere.* He thought of Kate and patted his vest pocket, making sure the little book was still there. It was the one thing he had taken from her belongings back at the cave. It was a peculiar book, leather bound and fastened with a small brass lock. He was resolved to find her again, once he made something of himself.

The snow was piling up, and the wind lashed. Even Thunder was slowing, struggling against the depth of it. With zero visibility, Silas had no idea where he was. The sky, land, horse, and rider were lost in whiteness. All of a sudden, Silas felt his horse perk up as if sensing something. He strained to see, but to no avail. The whipping winds shifted a bit and subsided slightly. Silas caught a whiff. *Smoke!* He was sure of it. "Come on, boy. Keeper her goin', Thunder boy. We're near ta somethin'. Maybe a shack." He trusted his faithful friend to lead them in the direction of the smoke, hopefully to shelter—friendly shelter.

There. He could see it now: light from windows, hazy at first, and then a little brighter as they closed the distance. A cabin. Silas called out, but his voice was barely audible. He climbed down off his horse, stiff and sore, but his faith beginning to revive.

A dog barked from inside the cabin, and the door opened a crack. "Who goes there?" a man with an accent called out.

"Me and my horse got lost in this here storm. Jest lookin' to hole up till it passes."

A woman came to the door and spoke something to the man. He opened the door wide and then said, "Come ahead."

The cabin, bigger than it first appeared, was warm, cheerful, and smelled of fresh-baked bread. The woman was Indian; her husband was a white man with dark hair and eyes. Silas figured he was French, from the sound of his accent. They had a passel of children. Two little dark-skinned boys, six and eight, clung to their mother, afraid of Silas. The woman held a dark-haired baby. In the kitchen area, two older girls looked up from the stove, eyes big with uncertainty, staring at the stranger standing in their home. The younger sister was dark like the boys and the baby. The other one, the oldest, looked altogether different from the rest. She was tall, pretty, with pale blond hair and blue eyes.

Chapter 9

Weeks turned into months, fall into winter, and business at Millie's Inn was at a standstill with traveling next to impossible. Wintry weather had hit harder than usual, with snow piling in drifts five feet high. When the last wagon load of supplies came in, the temporary help went out, leaving Millie, Henry, Max, Josh, Joey, Kate, Clayton and Johnny Boy, plus Freddie and Will, two young ranch-hands. Max and the boys, with the help of the workers, had stacked so much wood they swore they saw woodpiles in their sleep. They had butchered a pig, and Max had killed a buck, now hanging in the barn. The pantries were well stocked.

One stormy afternoon, Millie remembered that she had come across two magazines left by a guest: Peterson's *Ladies Magazine* and a mail-order catalog. Everyone was gathered around the fire: Clayton sleeping in his chair, Johnny Boy sprawled by his side, the boys carving small wooden animals with their blades, and everyone else dozing or reading. Kate prepared a pot of tea, and the two women pulled their chairs close to the fire, happy as they eagerly turned the pages of the magazines. "Oh, Kate, look at this lovely gown. It's the prettiest thing I've ever laid eyes on." Kate had to agree.

"And look at this one, Millie, with a matching cape!" exclaimed Kate.

"Oh my goodness sakes alive, would ya look at this one!" Millie said.

The boys had to get up off the floor and go take a peek at what all the fuss was about. Then they looked at each other and shook their heads. It didn't take them long to get back to the business of whittling.

Kate rested her head back. "Wonder if we'll ever get our trunks back: all my gowns, my winter coat, my diary, and Papa's things too." Then she went on to share with Millie the very strange way her mother's locket had shown up. "It's my most valued possession. Everything else can be replaced, but Mama's locket is all I have of her. And out of nowhere, it just showed up one day around the neck of an Indian!"

Kate glanced over at Max at the same time he looked up from his Bible. They exchanged a knowing look. She tried to focus on the magazine but still felt Max's eyes on her. She stole another peek and felt her cheeks grow warm. An unspoken message crossed between them: *I'll meet you here tonight.*

Millie interrupted her thoughts. "Oh, I declare. This is the one. Kate, look at this gorgeous sage-green velveteen with the little covered buttons and lace collar. You would look like a queen in this gown! I can picture it now." Kate laughed her irresistible laugh. Clayton snorted awake, and everyone else stirred, figuring they should brave the elements and get back to work.

Kate went downstairs early one March morning to find Millie gazing out the window, preoccupied, not aware anyone was near. Even from Millie's profile, Kate could tell she was downhearted, thinking about her Grace. "Millie?" Kate called out softly.

"Oh, mornin', honey," Millie said quickly, dabbing a hankie at her eyes. Kate moved closer and put an arm around her shoulder. Without speaking, they stood there together, looking out at nothing.

A late snowfall sparkled in the shimmering sunrise, not a track marking it. Everything ugly—the bare, muddy ground from yesterday—was covered in beauty, a present from God. Abruptly, Millie said, "Let's go for a walk!"

Kate was speechless. "Outside?"

"Of course outside. I'll get some boots and coats." She bustled off to gather a pile of warm clothing, mittens, scarves, and caps. Both women were tickled at themselves as they bundled until they could barely move and struggled to get out the door. As they trudged along arm in arm, their breath freezing in midair, they stumbled and laughed and nearly fell several times. They walked one direction and back again, not wanting to get too far from home, with Clayton still sleeping in his room.

"Ya know, Kate, I been thinkin'," Millie said. "After lookin' through those magazines, be a fine idea to put a mercantile next door and maybe build a church someday. Make this stop a real town."

Kate laughed brightly. "Millie Thatcher, you are amazing."

By the time they'd stomped the snow off their boots and gone back inside, they were sweltering but feeling wonderful. Millie and Kate had not only become friends, but Millie was like the mother Kate had missed for so much of her life. And Kate filled a spot of the hollowness in Millie's heart. They worked in the kitchen, side by side, and talked and prayed together often in Grace's room.

When Kate confessed her feelings for Max, Millie was not at all surprised. "Well, bless Pat," she said. "That's no wonder. We all knew you two were smitten when ya'll showed up here."

Kate blushed. "Could I ask you to pray for us, Millie? Max has been talking lately about Oregon, leaving when the weather changes. I'm worried the trip would be too much for Papa, but I won't leave him. Not ever again. I can't imagine going. And I can't imagine *not* going with Max and the boys. I love them, Millie, all three." She swallowed to keep from bursting into tears at the image of Max, Josh, and Joey riding away, heading west without her.

"Well, Kate, honey, seems to me you're borrowing from tomorrow. God's in control, sweetie. He knows the plans He has for you. Hand it over to Him, Kate. Leave it with Him."

———

It was a beautiful sunny day, still a bit nippy, but blue skies held a promise of spring just around the corner. The place was buzzing; everyone was pitching in to polish floors, wash windows, and get things in order for the busy travel season. Midafternoon, Kate took a few minutes to sit on the porch with her father. Their rocking chairs creaking and Johnny Boy's tail occasionally thumping the porch were the only sounds on that quiet afternoon. Suddenly Josh and Joey burst around the corner, one chasing the other, Kate not sure who was who. They were growing taller, their britches were too short, and their hair was too long. *Hmmm.* Kate had an idea.

In no time, she had a regular barbershop set up on the front porch. Josh drew the short straw and was first to climb up on the stool. Kate got down to business, and before long, clumps of golden locks were piled on the porch. When she finished, she combed his hair neatly and gently reminded him, "Next time in the bath, wash the back of your ears." Then Kate noticed behind his left ear a reddish spot about the size of her fingertip. "Joshua, did you know you have a birthmark?"

"Yes, ma'am. Mama said I was kissed by an angel so she could know us apart." Unnoticed, Millie was standing in the doorway. Josh went on, "And Joe's got one too!" He was grinning and looking over at Joey.

Joey, with teeth clenched and a scowl on his face, replied, "Don't say it, Josh."

Josh was giggling now. "The angel kissed him in a different place."

Joe's face turned beet red. *"Don't say it!* I'm warnin' you, Josh." His eyes bore holes into Josh, now cackling, holding his sides.

"It's all right, Joey," Kate interjected sweetly. "Nobody's out here but me, and I won't laugh." Yet she could hardly keep a straight face as she said it.

"The angel kissed him"—Josh could barely finish for laughing, "on the rump!"

Kate burst out laughing and pulled Joey into a warm hug. "To think, all this time you were foolin' me who was who. Now I know the secret to telling you boys apart." They all three laughed, and Johnny Boy barked, drawing their attention back toward Clayton. To Kate's amazement, her father, though looking down at his feet, was chuckling too.

Glancing over her shoulder for the first time, she noticed Millie, who was not laughing. In fact, she looked a bit pale and turned quickly to go back inside. That night, when the two women were alone, out of the blue Millie said, "She has a little red birthmark too. Gracie. On the bottom of her right foot. That's how I'll know for sure it's her. I can prove she belongs to me."

———

With the change in weather, coaches were arriving two or three a week, keeping the staff busy, at least in spurts. Kate was bustling around the dining room one morning, serving biscuits to diners, including Clayton and Max, who had missed the early breakfast prepared for hands. She was chatting with a couple from Missouri when she glanced across the room to see Max staring at her. She smiled, and he winked. Her cheeks warmed. She made her way to his table, filled his cup, and asked, "Anything else, Max?"

"As a matter of fact, yes. When you have a break, could you meet me on the porch?" He looked into his coffee. "I need to ask you something."

"Of course, Max, give me a few minutes." Her reply was a bit unsteady.

The cool, fresh air felt good as Kate made her way to the porch, where she found Max in a rocking chair. Johnny Boy raised his head, and his ears perked up. He was no doubt waiting for Clayton. Max stood, faced her, took off his hat, and started turning the brim in his hands.

"What is it, Max?"

"Well, I just wanted to ask, I mean, I wondered if it'd be all right, uh—"

"Just say it. I won't bite."

"I wondered, would you, uh—give me a haircut too?"

Kate broke out laughing. "Oh, Max! Certainly I will." She was still laughing, but she was a little disappointed. *Did you think he was going to propose? Don't be ridiculous, Kate. Just because you've shared a few kisses. Max is going to Oregon.* The thing she didn't know was that Max longed for her to become his bride; he prayed they could head west together and make their home in Oregon as a real family.

Stages came and went, going in both directions and bringing a wide variety of travelers, giving the kitchen crew much to talk about. There were businessmen and cowboys, emigrants and snooty ladies from the East. There were young and old, mixed-blood and full-blood Indians, and a sweet Chinese couple that, so grateful for the hospitality, gave Millie and Kate each a tin of tea leaves from China.

One especially peculiar little man, a loner who dressed meticulously in a black cutaway coat and bowler hat, with his round spectacles perched on the end of his nose, stayed two nights. He kept to himself, hardly speaking to others around him. He acted as if occupied with paperwork—this journal and that—but it was obvious to Millie and Kate that he was observing the goings-on in the dining room. And the most curious thing was that, instead of continuing west, he took the eastbound stage, back in the direction he came from. Very odd, but that's what kept things interesting.

Chapter 10

Clayton Alexander had been a successful cattle rancher and businessman in his prime. Until the horse accident, he had been the picture of health and strength, even as his hair began to gray. He was admired by fellow ranchers and looked up to by dignitaries of Kansas City.

When he lost his beloved wife, Clayton picked himself up, rising to the duty of bringing up four young daughters. He was a man of strong character and deep faith, a man of integrity. After recovering from a broken back, no longer able to ride, Clayton hired a crew to do the work he'd always done on the ranch and took a position with the bank in town. He also hired staff to help his housekeeper, Martha Smith, run the house, cook for the hands, and tutor the girls. Because of his keen business mind and character qualities, he brought clients—prominent men of sound financial status—to the bank. When Mr. Mosier, the president retired, Clayton was quickly promoted to fill the vacancy.

He and his girls were often invited to social events, which all but Kate savored. She was content to be home helping Martha, learning to cook and stitch. Liz, Ada, and Pearl became absorbed in high society, insisting on the latest styles, setting their caps for young men of higher station, climbing the social ladder by attending every party and social occasion in town, even if unaccompanied by their father.

At about that time, Clayton began forgetting things and was confused at times, recalling things that had never happened. Only Kate was aware of this strange behavior, but she thought it was due to long hours at the bank—the pressure of great responsibility. About eight months later, Clayton handed in his resignation, leaving the bank to "focus on obligations at home." He seemed to age before Kate's eyes, becoming less active and more easily agitated. He had provided for her, cared for her, making sure she and her sisters were well fed, well educated, and loved. She counted it a privilege to care for him and was devoted to doing so.

"You are wasting your life away, Kate!" Ada had exclaimed one day. "Don't you ever want to put on a pretty gown and go to the theater? Go dancing? You will end up an old maid and never amount to anything." Liz and Pearl had made their cutting remarks too, trying to convince her the old man should be committed to an asylum.

As days turned into months, Clayton seemed to lose his zeal for life. Only when he talked about his brothers, Clete and Charlie, who had gone west to Oregon, did his eyes light up, the old sparkle returning. At seventeen, Kate began formulating a plan. She wouldn't do anything rash. She took her idea before the Lord in prayer. Her mother had taught her at a very young age to pray about everything and to trust Jesus for the right path. She would pray every day about taking her dear father to Oregon.

Now there they were, stranded in a way, between home and Oregon. Kate felt sure it was all part of whatever God planned for them. After all, hadn't she prayed? She certainly could see God's hand in all that had happened, how He had brought her through time and again. "But what's next, Lord?" she whispered.

Clayton had dozed off in the rocking chair, Johnny Boy at his side. *If only I could communicate with him the way I used to,* she thought. *The way we talked sometimes in the evenings before—*

"Papa?" Kate drew her chair up close to his. "I'm so confused, Papa." She reached for his hand, and he stirred. "I need your help.

I need your advice." From the other side of the kitchen door, Max heard her voice, and though it was barely audible, he could feel her anxiety as she spoke with her father. He couldn't help but lean in to hear.

"I don't know what to do about Max and the boys, Papa. They were so eager to get to Oregon, and well on their way. Then *I* came along." She paused. Max heard her sniff and knew she was crying. It was killing him not to burst through the door and take her in his arms. "I love him, Papa. I'm in love with Max. And the boys. I love those boys. Oh, Papa, I won't ever leave you again. And I won't compromise your health and safety by taking you west."

Once more there was silence. She was crying again, and Max felt a tear roll down his own cheek. He whispered to the back of the door, "I love you too, Katy. God knows I've loved you from the start."

Kate blew her nose, dabbed at her eyes, and sat straighter. Even though her father couldn't understand, telling him felt better—at least a little bit. And then, to her astonishment and to Max's on the other side of the door, Clayton chuckled his old familiar chuckle and said, as plain as day, "We're goin' to Oregon, Katy. Yes, we are. And we're takin' this here hound dog with us."

The dining room was a buzz of preparation for the afternoon stagecoach, which would be arriving soon from the east. Kate had cooked and cleaned all morning but with lighter steps and a song in her heart, praising God and thanking Him for so many blessings. That night she would tell Max the news that she and Papa would go to Oregon with him. In one of Clayton's lucid moments, God had answered her prayer.

The tables were set, and the aroma of baking bread and simmering stew permeating the whole building. The floor was polished and windows shined, and though the air was still nippy, it was the start of the busy season: spring in Eastern Idaho.

"Here they come!" shouted the boys as the coach slowed to a stop, stirring up a cloud of dust.

Voices grew louder, women's voices, angry women's voices. "What a dreadful trip! And this dust is going to ruin my dress."

Another voice said, "We've been crammed in with these awful smelly people for days! I'm going to order a hot bath immediately."

And then another: "Well, I want food first! We've nearly starved to death on this frightful trip. Ohhh, get away, you mangy old dog."

They complained their way up the steps and burst through door, a blaze of color turning every head. One of these cranky ladies from back east wore deep-purple taffeta, one a bright yellow, and the other red silk, all with coordinating stylish hats; plumes and frills galore.

Kate was frozen in place. Her mouth opened, but she couldn't speak. There, standing in all their glory, were Liz, Ada, and Pearl, her sisters.

Kate finally spoke, her voice shaky. "How did you—"

"How did we find you?" Ada snapped. She was the most outspoken, although one could barely tell between the three.

"You had no right to take Papa." Liz blurted out without sparing the drama. "We hired a Pinkerton detective. That's how we found out, and we're here to take Papa home."

Pearl chimed in. "We know what you're up to, Kate, keeping us from our rightful inheritance."

During the confrontation, their father sat unblinking by the fire. His daughters did not even acknowledge his presence. The tension in the room was thick, and Kate was trying hard to keep from collapsing in a heap of tears. *Be strong and courageous.*

Max heard the ruckus, slipped up next to Kate, and took her hand in his. A smudgy little face popped up between them and then another, next to Kate, taking her other hand. The kitchen door flung open, and Millie, with her usual cheerfulness and grace, erupted into the room. "Well, who have we here? Such lovely young ladies!"

Kate tried to regain her composure. "Uh—these are my—my sisters, Millie. May I introduce Liz, Pearl, and Ada Alexander." Turning toward her sisters, she added, "Uh, this is the inn's proprietress, Millie Thatcher."

Millie acknowledged each lady with charm and then sashayed over to Clayton's side, put her arm affectionately around his shoulders, and kissed the top of his head. Without skipping a beat, she declared with dramatic flair, "How wonderful! You girls are here just in time for the wedding."

"Wedding?" the sisters said in unison. And for a moment all three were speechless.

Ada rushed to Clayton's chair and knelt before him. "Is it true, Papa? Is there going to be a wedding?" He just stared at her without recognition. "Answer me, Papa. Is there going to be a wedding?"

Kate wanted to protect him from her uncaring sisters. She started toward them, but Max drew her back, tightening the hold on her hand.

Clayton pinched the bridge of his nose like he had a bad headache. "Yes," he said clearly, "and then we go."

"Go? Go where? Where are you going?" Ada persisted.

"Why, Oregon, of course."

Millie hurried the girls along to their room, suggesting they rest and take a little time to freshen up before dinner. She showed them to a corner suite with two large featherbeds, her best room— whatever it took to get them out of the dining room and to give Kate a chance to recover. Kate had been as white as a sheet when Millie interrupted, having heard the conversation from behind the kitchen door.

In the meantime, Max pulled Kate into his arms, willing her to quit shaking. "I'm sorry about the whole thing, Katy, but we won't let them take your father. I promise that will not happen." He tenderly brushed the tears from her cheeks as she sank into him, gathering strength. As only Kate could, she suddenly began to giggle, pressing her forehead against Max's chest. He wasn't sure if she was laughing or crying.

"Did you see the look on their faces?" She was laughing full out now. "Millie truly played the part. They really think Papa and Millie are getting married!" The boys were still right in the middle of things, giggling because Kate was giggling, which made Max chime in with his own deep laughter.

"I sure hope the Lord forgives Millie for fibbin'!" she added.

Max could only hope and pray that there *would* be a wedding. His and Miss Kate Alexander's.

Chapter 11

Dinner was tense, but they got through it, Kate keeping to the kitchen as much as possible and sending Sarah out to serve the guests. After dinner, the sisters stayed in their room. Kate figured they were more than likely plotting ways to kidnap their father, which would be essentially impossible. The stagecoach would be their only getaway, they had no other options.

At supper that night, Ada announced in a snooty way, "We will be canceling our reservation on the eastbound stage tomorrow, as we have decided to stay for the wedding." Kate choked on her cobbler and scrambled to come up with some reason they shouldn't wait for the wedding—especially since there *was* no wedding.

She had joined her sisters for dessert, hoping to ease the friction and gain courage to ask their forgiveness for absconding with their father in the first place. Max walked by, a mug of coffee in his hand, headed for the front door. She glanced his way and caught the message in his deep-brown eyes that said, *Meet me on the porch.*

The three irritable girls decided to sleep on their decision to forgive or not and said their good nights. With a sigh of relief, Kate grabbed her shawl and headed out to the porch.

Having completed their chores for the day, Josh and Joey went to their secret hideout in the barn out back. It was dusk, but they still had enough light to play for a bit before heading to the bunkhouse.

"Boy, I'd never believe them mean women are related to Kate," said Joey.

"Me neither," replied Josh. "All that face paint and them feathers stickin' outa their hats? They ain't nothin' like Kate."

"They just came to make trouble, Joe. And the sooner they git, the better."

The boys worked on their fort a while then went down the ladder when it was too dark to see. The bunkhouse was lit up as some of the hands unlaced their boots, getting ready to turn in. Of course they knew Max was with Kate, probably snuggled up on the porch. The boys climbed into their bedrolls and were just about to blow out the lamp when Josh spotted a huge spider walking up the wall.

"Hey, Joey, looky there! That's the biggest ol' spider I ever seen. It would scare—"

They looked at each other, and without words, formed a plan. By the time they found a jar with a lid, the spider was almost out of reach, but they stacked one cot on top of the other and got it.

Quietly, they slipped their boots back on and crept out the door and across to the back porch of the inn, through the kitchen, and up the stairs, holding their breath at every creak. Light from the lamps still burned in the corner suite, sending a shaft of light out beneath the door. So far so good.

The spider was very cooperative; once the lid was removed, it gladly escaped under the door. Continuing with their unspoken plan, the boys slipped quietly down the stairs and hid beneath them to wait. This was a place they had hidden often, because no one could see them as they observed the entire dining room through a crack in the stairs.

They waited. Nothing. They wondered if those women weren't the scared type and had simply stepped on it. They waited. Joey yawned.

Suddenly, all fury broke loose: screaming that could wake the dead. The three sisters got stuck trying to get through the door all at once and, finally free, flew down the stairs in a state of hysterics. Josh and Joey had to clamp their hands over their mouths. The whole place erupted: Millie tearing down the stairs with a lamp, Max and Kate bursting through the front door and lighting another. Even Henry heard the commotion and came hobbling in. At the site of everyone staring at them, Ada, Pearl, and Liz bunched together and started the screaming all over again. It was a sight to behold in their corsets and bloomers.

The next morning, Ada, Pearl, and Liz didn't make an appearance at breakfast. All three had slept in one bed and kept the lamps burning all night. The boys were making their way through the kitchen, headed out to chores after a hearty breakfast, when Josh noticed a pan of leftover biscuits and reached for one.

Sarah's sweet voice cautioned, "No, boys. Sorry, but Millie said to keep those warm, along with some gravy and scrambled eggs, for Miss Kate's sisters."

"Oh, that's all right, Miss Sarah. We're pretty full anyway."

When Sarah left the kitchen to finish clearing breakfast dishes, Josh turned to Joey with that look in his eye. "No, Josh, we can't be stealin' biscuits."

"That's not what I was thinkin', Joe." Immediately Joe caught on. His eyes sparkled with mischief. They hurried to the pantry, and there on the top shelf was just what they had in mind: cayenne pepper. Joey gave Josh a leg up, who could just barely reach the tin with the tips of his fingers.

"Hurry, Josh!" They stopped to listen for Sarah or anyone else that might be coming, but luckily they were still alone in the kitchen. Quickly Josh poured cayenne pepper into the eggs, while Joey stirred. For good measure, they decided with a look, to sprinkle some in the gravy too.

Eventually, the three ladies made their way downstairs, dressed in gowns equally as stylish and colorful as yesterday's, their hair piled in heaps of curls and ribbons.

"No wonder they missed breakfast," whispered Joey. The boys were back under the stairs, eagerly awaiting that first bite. Sarah had nearly caught them switching water glasses, but they'd managed just in the nick of time. It took those gals a long time to finally take a bite. Liz had a mouthful, and she began to fan her face, her eyes opening wider. Before Ada and Pearl realized what was happening, they had shoveled a spoonful into their own mouths. Suddenly all three were spitting out their food, jumping up and down, knocking over chairs, and screaming for water. Kate and Sarah rushed into the dining room. Not knowing for sure what happened, they began throwing pitchers of water over the women, virtually ruining their hairdos.

Still spitting and coughing, their curls and ribbons drooping and dresses sagging, the sisters hurried up the stairs, screaming and crying. "We've gotta get out of here!" Liz sputtered. "This is the most dreadful place I've ever seen."

The boys shook hands, beaming at their success. "We didn't even *need* to sprinkle on them dog hairs."

The following morning, without taking a chance on breakfast, the three ladies settled in porch rockers and waited for the eastbound stage. They were finely dressed as always, but had taken it down a notch; the three sisters just wanted to get away, the sooner the better. Kate quietly joined them, sitting in a fourth rocker. None of the sisters spoke; they just looked straight ahead into the overcast day.

"I suppose we're in for rain," Ada offered, barely audible.

Liz chimed in, "Of course it's going to rain. We're sure to get stuck in the mud. Everything else has gone wrong on this horrendous trip." She shot a sideways glance at Kate.

"Look, girls," Kate said. "I'm terribly sorry about what's happened these past two days, but they're just boys. They were looking out for me, thinking they were doing the right thing by"—she paused, swallowed, then continued, "getting rid of you."

All three turned toward Kate with incredulous looks on their painted faces. "The boys? Why, those little devils!" Pearl said, angry tears pooling in her eyes. "That's what they are, those bad naughty boys. This isn't over, Kathryn. We will be back with reinforcements! You had no right, no right—oh, never mind." She burst into tears.

"Listen, Pearl, and Ada and Liz too," Kate said. "I was wrong. I should never have taken Papa away behind your backs. Please forgive me. It's just—I thought he might get better if he could see his brothers; it's what he wanted more than anything. I couldn't bear the thought of him spending the rest of his life in an asylum."

Liz broke in. "Well, it's not such a bad place, Kate. After all, you can visit on Wednesdays and Sunday afternoons. For heaven's sake, you act like we're horrible daughters. We only want the best for Papa too, you know."

Kate was wiping away a single tear, feeling torn, wanting to do the right thing. Johnny Boy started to bark inside, and Millie appeared on the porch. "Stage is a'comin'. Right on schedule for once." That's when Millie realized she'd walked into a strained situation. "Why you girls sittin' out here with your travel bags? Stage won't be goin' anywhere till after breakfast tomorrow." Their three faces went pale. Millie glanced at Kate, needing to be rescued. "Katy, would ya give me a hand in the kitchen, darlin'?"

After a long, restless night for everybody, the three sisters boarded the eastbound coach and left as they had come, in a cloud of dust, dramatically complaining until they could no longer be heard.

Kate stayed by Clayton's side most of the day, worried he would realize his three girls had gone without saying good-bye. But he just dozed, occasionally patting the old dog by his side. He seemed content, and that's all Kate asked—and prayed for. *Lord, may he be content and feel loved, whatever happens.*

Chapter 12

Max had promised Josh and Joey they could take Henry's old sorrel and go to the fishing hole a couple of miles downstream from the creek out back, once their chores were done. The boys loved it there, loved to explore, catch frogs, and fish from the bank.

By late afternoon, as the sun was going down, they were excited to take their string of trout, nine in all, back to the kitchen in time for supper. They climbed up on old Dan and headed for home. Since there was more than one way to get there, they chose to take the higher trail. It was difficult to navigate, but that made it more of an adventure.

Dan bobbed along as if bored by the whole journey, but he was surefooted and cooperative with both boys on his back.

Thinking he heard something in the brush, Josh pulled on the reigns and brought Dan to a stop. Both boys looked in every direction. Nothing. They moved on a bit, then heard it again. "Think it's a bear?" Joey whispered.

"Naw, Dan would be actin' up."

"Well, he's twenty-seven years old, probably couldn't act up if he wanted."

There it was again, like a moaning sound from the downhill side.

"Over there," Josh said. "There's somethin' or somebody in them bushes!" Josh and Joey both were getting skittish, to say the least. "I think someone's hurt," he added.

"Do ya think we should take off then?" Joe suggested. "Get help?"

Josh pondered the idea and then gave Joe that knowing look, the one when they read each other's mind. "Yeah, I know. The Good Samaritan." Their father had read the Bible every night after supper, and even though they were little tykes at the time, those stories had stuck with them. They knew they had to stop, even if scared stiff.

They both slid off Dan, trusting he would just stand there, and gingerly crept closer to the sound they had heard. Barely breathing, they cautiously moved closer and closer until suddenly Joe's foot came within two inches of an arm. Simultaneously, the boys stifled a scream, clapping their hands over their mouths.

Warily they pushed back the sagebrush, exposing the rest of a bronze body, face down in a pool of blood. This time they couldn't hold back the identical yelp coming from their identical mouths. "A dead Indian! Now what do we do?" Joe said. Just as Josh was about to say he didn't have any idea, a moan came from the Indian and his arm moved slightly.

"Bless Pat! He ain't dead," Joe said, and Josh gave the arm a little poke.

"He's hurt serious, Joe. We got to get him on Dan somehow and take him with us."

"What if he's a bad Indian?"

"That don't matter. He's lost lots of blood. He couldn't harm us if he tried."

The boys led the horse as close as possible and used all the strength in them to load the young Indian across Dan's back, being careful of his shoulder, which they could now see had taken a bullet. They also saw something else. Tied to the beaded leather around the Indian's neck dangled a yellow plume. The feather had been an unmistakable feature of Pearl's stylish hat.

———

Silas knew he'd hit one of them.

From his vantage point in the higher elevation, he'd seen the aftermath of a stage robbery by a band of renegade Indians. They had disappeared into the nearby forest with what looked to be some of the women passengers, obviously struggling against their captors. Silas was too far away, but he fired shots in their direction to try and scare them into letting the ladies go.

Two young braves had remained to rummage through the trunks atop the stagecoach, while the driver and another man were tied up back to back. The two Indians disappeared into the shadows of the ravine beneath him. Silas had stayed put behind a boulder, watching the scene unfold, wary of the two that disappeared somewhere below him.

Suddenly arrows began to fly by each side of his protective rock. He tossed his hat on top of the boulder to his right and waited until it took an arrow that blew it off the rock. Quick as a cat, he leaped out to the left of his shield, firing his rifle until one brave ran off, mounted his paint horse in a single leap, and raced into the woods. The other dropped to the ground below and didn't move.

Silas was very close to the old mine where Boss claimed to have stashed a shipment of government gold. It was part of his plan of restitution, returning everything he knew had been stolen, even if it meant jail time. He was a changed man, redeemed and saved by grace, thanks to Jesus—and Kate. He still carried her leather journal in his vest pocket. He knew he'd find her someday. At the moment, though, he needed to make a decision. Keep on the trail to the mine? Or track the Indians that had those women.

He had to do what he could and trust God to keep them safe until he figured out how to rescue them. Silas was feeling his age, but he had to try. *Lord, help me, Jesus.*

"Jumpin' Jehoshaphat! Lawdy, Lawdy! Thought you young'uns went fishin' fo' *fish*!" Henry was first to see the boys come through the back gate, avoiding the view from the inn. They didn't want Kate and Millie to see they had brought home a half-dead Indian, especially with the yellow feather. Henry directed them to lay the wounded brave on his bunk and then commenced to tie his feet together with a leather strap and his one good arm to the bedpost. The Indian grunted and groaned then passed out again. After instructing Josh and Joey to fetch a small jug of whiskey and his doctoring bag, Henry was ready to dig out the bullet and sew up the wound.

The boys raced out to find Max, taking the yellow feather with them. Of all the bad luck, Kate was with him, watching him shoe a horse. "Hey, Max," Josh hollered. "Can ya c'mere for a minute?"

Max glanced their way. "Gotta get this ol' boy ready for the next stage. You fellas walk on over here."

Kate chimed in, "Brought some warm cookies out. You two are just in time." Josh quickly stuffed the yellow plume down Joe's pant leg, and reluctantly the two walked across the dusty ground to where Max was working away. Kate, with her beautiful big smile, held out the basket of warm ginger cookies.

It didn't take long for Max to see something was wrong. Josh had a sort of scowl on his face, and Joey's chin was quivering. Max stopped his work. "What's happened? I know somethin's wrong, boys, so fess up. What'd ya do?"

Josh looked at the ground. Joey sniffed, reached down his pant leg, and pulled out the now limp, dirty, and bloody yellow feather. "Something really bad happened, Max." Joey began to cry and looked up at Kate. "Indians got your sisters, ma'am. This here yeller feather is all that's left."

Kate reached for the feather with one hand and clutched her chest with the other. "Oh dear God!" Then she fainted dead away.

Chapter 13

Max hollered at Freddie and Will to saddle horses for the three of them, and they rode like the wind to the place Josh and Joe had described, continuing east until they came upon the stagecoach. The two men were still tied up. "Them lowdown Shoshones run off with the supplies shipment and three women passengers. They went thata way, into them timbers."

Max and company turned their horses in that direction. "Hey, wait a minute. Ain't ya gonna untie us?" Quickly Max cut them free and took off in a squall of dust as the three raced toward the woods. Once in the dense forest, they slowed to a walk, eventually finding the trail, and tracked as best they could the band of hard-to-track Indians.

All three heard it at the same time and came to a standstill. "What was that?" Freddie whispered.

Will shuddered. "Sounds like wildcats caught in a trap."

They moved in slowly, the woman's screeching becoming clearer. And clearer. "This hat cost a small fortune, and look at it now!"

"Well, at least you still have a hat!" another screeched.

"Those fancy hats are the least of our worries. Be glad ya still have hair on your heads."

In unison, the women broke into tears, wailing.

"You're right about them bein' wildcats," said Max. "It's Kate's sisters, sure as the world."

Max devised a plan: tying their horses to nearby trees, spreading out and creeping as noiselessly as possible, inching toward the sounds. The sisters were huddled together on a log off to the side of a clearing, which had been the Indians' campsite. Oddly, the young braves were ignoring the women and listening intently to a tall, rugged-looking mountain man with a leather patch over one eye.

Max strained to listen but couldn't catch much of the conversation. The big man seemed to be speaking their native language, gesturing toward the women off and on, who were still wailing away, sitting on the log. The Indians were noticeably thin.

Max signaled to the other men to move in slowly, carefully, holding their fire unless he motioned otherwise. The big man pulled a pistol from his holster and, with a bit of ceremony, unloaded it, letting each bullet spill to the ground. The Indian then pulled an arrow from his quiver and, with a bit of ceremony, broke it in half. They had made an agreement. Two of the Indians leaped on their horses while the big man with one eye stepped in his stirrup and heaved himself up on his horse, leaving the women under the watch of three skinny braves.

Meanwhile, back at the inn, the boys were keeping very busy looking after Kate and then the wounded Indian. Then they went back inside to fetch a cup of tea for Kate, then another for the Indian. They were to "look after everyone," Max had said. Of course, Millie was overseeing the looking-after.

The young brave was still groggy and keeping his eyes slanted toward Henry, who sat on a pile of hay close by, reading the Bible. "What good'll it do, Henry?" Joey asked sweetly. "Reckon he don't understand a single word yer sayin'."

Henry peered over his spectacles, the lines around his eyes smiling up at the boys. "Maybe he don't. But ah sho do. Yessah. Ah sho nuff do." He directed the boys to sit a spell and listen too.

71

It was a hundred wonders a war didn't break out when Silas spotted the parade of color coming right at him, weaving their way through the thick forest. The women on horseback were being led by three cowboys. Silas's two companions took off like bullets—like the ones he no longer had in his gun. He had just made a bargain with the Shoshone, exchanging grain, cornmeal, and jerky for the three women. How would he ever rescue them a second time? Other than the knife in his boot, he was defenseless; the odds were against him.

The women recognized Silas just as Max drew his gun. "Good heavens, Max, don't shoot the poor man!" declared Ada. "He was trying to free us from those savage Indians!"

Max lowered his pistol to shut the irritating women up, if for no other reason. "Is that right, mister? What the lady said?"

Silas scratched at the stubble on his chin. "That's the only business I have here. I'd like to make mention though, them so-called savages ain't bad Injuns. They don't mean no harm. They's just hungry."

———

"Wounded Eagle," as the boys had named him (sounded better than Wounded Yellow Feather) was very hungry. Millie said to start him out with tea and a little bread. Then he gobbled up the ginger cookies the boys had slipped to him. So they brought a bowl of stew, followed by more ginger cookies. Henry said he'd be well in no time at that rate.

It seemed Wounded Eagle was intrigued with Josh and Joey. His deep-brown eyes never left their identical faces as he was sopping up the stew with thick slices of bread. He had been untied and had his feet slung over the edge of the bed. Henry continued to read the Bible, periodically shaking his head at the wonder of it, saying soft amens.

Millie helped Kate to the dining room, where Clayton dozed by the fire. Johnny Boy dozed too, right by the old man's side. Kate settled in the rocking chair next to him, trying to pray away the feeling of dread that consumed her. *It's my fault, Lord. Everything that's happened. If it's not too late, Lord, I pray that no harm comes to my sisters.*

Johnny Boy's ears perked up, and though he was too lazy to move, he gave a low bark. Horses were coming. Soon Kate heard them and ran to the porch. Even though their gowns, vivid in the distance gave Kate instant relief, she was more relieved to make out Max, leading the pack. He and the two hands led the three horses toting Liz, Ada, and Pearl. *Thank you, Lord!*

Then her eyes caught a forth horseman, lagging back. She started walking toward the bedraggled party, curious about the big man in back. As her sisters were being helped off their horses, Kate picked up her pace, vowing to receive them with affection. But with a sudden recognition, she passed them by, even running past Max and right into the big man's bear hug. "Silas!" "Miss Kate!" A tear escaped his one good eye, as her tears were spilling over.

———

In the days ahead, a spirit of penance and forgiveness, of grace, seemed to permeate the household. Kate and her sisters talked late into the night. The girls began to pay attention to their father, and he rewarded them every now and then with recognition: a faint smile. Millie organized a Bible study that began with the women, but soon Silas got the menfolk to be part of it too.

So they gathered after supper until one whole end of the dining room was filled—all the wonderful people Kate had begun to think of as family. Even Wounded Eagle, with reluctance, came one evening with Henry. They sat off a bit from the group, and Josh and Joey left their front-row floor space to sit with them. After all, the old black man, the young Indian, and the two freckle-faced, blond boys had formed a treaty of sorts, an alliance shaped by growing trust. Because Silas had some native language skills, he befriended the Indian too—the very one he had shot and left for dead.

Late one evening, Kate and Max finally had a moment to themselves as they stayed behind to ready the dining room for morning. "Katy? Wanta sit with me a bit?"

Her smile met his. "I'll get the coffee." They were very comfortable with each other, just sitting side by side, quietly gazing into the fire. "Isn't it wonderful, Max, the way God is working things out? It's a miracle how He's reaching Liz and Pearl and Ada too. Truly a miracle." Max just listened. "If only we could've made it to Oregon. I've failed Papa, because that's what he wanted most of all. Deep in my heart, I know we'll never make it."

Max was filled with mixed emotions. Oregon, the land of milk and honey. With all the commotion around there, he'd actually forgotten about Oregon. There was much to do. He needed to get back to work on the wagon he was building, back to where they'd left off in August. It seemed so long ago; so much had happened.

"Max?" He blinked, realizing Kate had been speaking. "I was commenting how Papa's health has failed since we left Kansas last summer. He's grown weaker, less coherent, and his cough worsened during the night. I won't leave him again. And he certainly couldn't make the trip to Oregon. I know that now." She suddenly looked very tired.

"Kate, you, more than anyone, have cared for your father, made sure he was comfortable and content. You have loved him with such unselfish love. Does it really matter if he gets to Oregon? I mean, if you're with people you love, who love you back, it doesn't matter where you are." Though his noble counsel was spoken for Kate's benefit, a sudden reality hit him. It was as if God was whispering his own words back to him. *Does it really matter where you are, Max? Would he and the boys find a better life in Oregon? Better than this?*

"Kate?"

"Yes, Max?" She turned to face him, her eyes seeking his in the soft glow of the hearth.

"Kate." He was sure she could hear his heartbeat. Her heart skipped a beat too. "Katy, darlin', will you marry me?" He dropped to one knee before her. "Will you be my wife, Katy?"

"Oh, Max!"

"I don't care if we ever go west. I love you, Kate, right here."

Kate brushed away a tear and took a deep breath. "Yes, Max! Yes, yes, yes! I love you too, Max Reed. You are a gift from God."

He stood, pulled her to her feet, and drew her into his strong embrace. "Oh, my sweet, sweet Katy." Tenderly they kissed and then again with deep yearning. They held each other, relishing the moment, both grateful to God above.

A sudden clanking from the kitchen brought them to attention. Kate smoothed back her tangled hair.

"Who's there?" Max hollered. The kitchen door creaked open. In the lamplight, in their long johns, stood Josh, Joe, and Wounded Eagle.

Conscious of the late hour, Joey whispered, "Wounded Eagle wants a cookie."

A deep voice followed from behind him. "Cooo-keee."

Max and Kate burst out laughing.

Chapter 14

Millie was all over it. The circuit preacher was coming through April 24, just three weeks away. She had wired him that there would be a wedding to perform and asked if he could pick up her order from the Dawson City mercantile along the way. Then she set to sewing, reworking the most conservative option Ada had in her trunk. It was a pale-pink taffeta gown trimmed in black. Removing the black was a huge improvement, and adding white lace to the bodice, the hem of the sleeves, and an overlay on the billowing skirt completed the desired effect. Never mind that the dining room would need new curtains.

Millie nipped here and tucked there so that the dress fit Kate's petite figure. She delegated assignments to the whole crew, thankful the heavy travel season hadn't yet begun. Kate and Sarah busied themselves in the kitchen, planning the wedding feast with Tom the cook and making candles for decorating, as it was a bit too early for wildflowers. She wasn't sure what Max was doing; she hadn't seen much of him since the day he proposed. In fact, during the day, she didn't see much of the boys either, or Silas, for that matter. Or even Wounded Eagle. Max said he had natural ability with the wild horses they had corralled, so she thought perhaps he'd ridden off on one.

It was the happiest day of Kate's life. She couldn't believe the image in the mirror—*her* image. The wedding dress was more beautiful than any gown she had ever seen in any women's magazine. Liz's white doeskin slippers were closest to her size and soft, with a dozen tiny buttons on each. A single white chiffon flower had been removed from Pearl's favorite hat and pinned to the side of Kate's elegant twist, which the girls had arranged, leaving tendrils of soft curls to frame her lovely face. She gently caressed her mother's locket, the finishing touch.

All of a sudden, she heard the strains of Henry's fiddle. *It's time.* As she walked to the stairway leading down to the dining room, down to her future with Max, she couldn't help but whisper a prayer of thanksgiving to the Lord. At the foot of the stairs, dressed in new white shirts, their hair slicked back and faces scrubbed, stood her escorts, Josh and Joe. She let out a little chuckle as they properly held their elbows out, one on each side of her. *How I love these boys!* she thought.

As the three slowly walked up the aisle, between tables and chairs that had been shoved back, Kate could barely see for the tears pooling in her eyes. Awaiting her were all the ones she loved. Her father was in his rocking chair, dressed in Dallas Thatcher's finest, Johnny Boy at his side.

Millie, her blue eyes bright with tears, looked at Kate with all the pride of a mother. Liz, Ada, and Pearl, dressed in lovely gowns with softer makeup and hairstyles than usual, were smiling sweetly. Pearl dabbed her eyes with a hanky. Kate thought, *will they ever forgive Josh and Joey for the spider and hot pepper episodes?*

And there stood Silas, looking at her with a heart of love. To think it all started when he hijacked the stage and kidnapped her. She swallowed back a laugh. *Will he ever forgive me for calling him a yellow-bellied sidewinder?*

Wounded Eagle was next, smiling broadly, his white teeth gleaming. *I guess he didn't run off after all.*

In the middle of the assembly, Max stood straight in a store-bought coat of dark blue. His broad shoulders and tanned face against the crisp white shirt made him extra handsome. He was the love of her life, and God had tossed her right into his lap. He had protected her and cared for her. He had given up Oregon for her.

Just as the preacher opened his Bible, Joey leaned over to Kate to whisper something. His comment caused her to look beyond Max and the minister to the mantel. Josh and Joey watched her intently as recognition dawned. A dozen or more candles in different shapes and sizes flickered there. Right in the middle stood a rustic cross, obviously hand whittled. Kate squatted down to their level, her gown poofing up all around them. The preacher cleared his throat in a "let's get on with it" way.

"Did you two whittle that cross?" Kate whispered.

Josh commenced to explain, forgetting to whisper. "I made the long part, and Joe whittled the cross piece, and Wounded Eagle tied it together with leather." Kate couldn't hold it in. She did her laughing-crying thing, pulling the boys to her. "We were in charge of decorations," they said in unison.

"It's the best decoration in the whole world!" Kate exclaimed, and she meant it.

Finally, she stood to face Max, glowing. They said their vows, and he slipped a ring on her finger. Millie's ring.

"I now pronounce you"— the preacher didn't get a chance to finish before Josh said, "Ain't ya gonna kiss her?"

"Yeah," Joey chimed in. "We already seen ya do it on the porch." Everyone, including the preacher, laughed, but Max was dead serious when he kissed Kate.

"It is now my pleasure to introduce Mr. and Mrs. Jeremiah Maxwell Reed," the preacher announced with flair, and the crowd clapped and cheered. Henry immediately launched into a jaunty tune on the fiddle as Millie and Sarah dashed to the kitchen, where the aroma had become more tantalizing with each passing hour.

The celebration continued into the evening as all feasted on elk roast, potatoes, carrots, onions, gravy, cornbread, and biscuits. Millie had baked applesauce cake and buttermilk pies. Everyone danced, including Kate's sisters, taking turns with the boys and Silas and even Wounded Eagle.

In the excitement, Max danced Kate right out the front door into the chilly April dusk. They didn't notice the cold a bit as he kissed her soundly then kissed her again. "It's about time to go home, Mrs. Reed."

She threw her head back and laughed. "We have a home?" *Surely he doesn't mean the bunkhouse,* she thought. "Well, before we go home, our guests are expecting us to open presents."

Everyone had a gift for the happy couple: embroidered pillowcases, handmade soap, Josh and Joey's cross. The sisters gave Clayton's gold watch to Max. Wounded Eagle gave his beaded headband to Kate. Then slowly Silas walked over to her. He reached inside his vest, taking his time to remove her leather journal, the one part of her that had kept him going, given him strength. Whenever he had been tempted to give up or give in to the devil, he would place his hand on that little book, right over his heart, and remember her words and her beautiful voice. *Amazing grace, how sweet the sound that saved a wretch like me.*

———

Though the April night was chilly, bright moonlight made it magical. Solomon, without a saddle, stood patiently while Max settled his bride in front of him on the horse's back. "Max, where are we going?" Kate said. "I hope your idea of a honeymoon is not a campsite in the woods."

Max chuckled. "Well, with everyone giving presents, I just remembered I have a present too." She leaned back into him, her pink taffeta and lace like a cloud. "Oh, and one more thing; hold on now." He slipped the silk neckerchief from his collar and blindfolded Kate with it.

"Max! Whatever are you doing?"

He clicked his tongue, and Solomon responded by bobbing his head and walking along to who knew where. After several minutes, Max reined the horse to a stop. He helped Kate down and turned her in a certain direction before removing the neckerchief.

It took a second for her eyes to adjust, but there in the moonlight, nestled in a grove of cottonwoods, she saw a little log cabin with lamplight in the windows, smoke gently winding its way from the chimney. Kate's mouth opened, but she couldn't speak. *This is where he's been! And the boys and Silas too, and Wounded Eagle!* Kate had been stifling tears almost all day, but she could no longer hold them back. She burst into sobbing, laughing, hugging, and kissing.

"Oh, Max, it's the most—*sniff*—beautiful—*sniff*—wonderful—*sniff*— sight I've ever, ever seen."

Max pulled her close. "Welcome home, Katy. Welcome home."

Chapter 15

Clayton passed away in September, just five months after the wedding, his four daughters at his side. The following spring, May 10 to be exact, Jeremiah Alexander Reed came into the world, the spitting image of Josh and Joe, and the joy of his parents' life. Everyone on the place felt akin to that precious baby, especially "Grandma" Millie. The boys were crazy about their little brother, though technically he was their nephew. They loved to make him goo and giggle. They also dubbed him Jake, and it stuck.

Since that April night when Max surprised Kate with their cozy cabin, he had added a porch, dug a well, and ordered a cook stove, which had finally arrived. With a pie in the oven, chicken and dumplings simmering, and a baby in her arms, Kate thought she must be in heaven.

It appeared to everyone that Silas hung around Millie an awful lot, and Millie didn't seem to object. They often took their evening coffee on the porch, contentedly seated in the rockers Kate and Max once occupied—the very spot Josh and Joey saw Max steal a kiss. They talked and rocked until late into the night, sharing their life, their hopes and dreams. Eventually, it was only natural for Millie to tell Silas about Gracie K. Silas grew quiet and thoughtful. He continued that way the remainder of the evening, but Millie didn't think much of it.

It seemed peculiar early the next morning that Silas did not come in for breakfast—not even coffee. Millie grabbed her shawl and ran out to the bunkhouse, afraid he might be ill. But he was gone, along with his horse, his bedroll, and his few meager belongings. "Freddy? Will?" she called out. "Have you seen Silas this mornin'?"

Freddy came around the corner. "Well, ma'am, he had to go. I mean, he had business to take care of, Miss Millie."

Millie couldn't believe it. "Did he say when he'd be back? Where he was headed?"

"No, ma'am. I don't know."

"Thank you, Freddy," she said, trying to act indifferent, and walked back toward the kitchen. Her shoulders sagged. *I can't believe he would leave without tellin' me. I thought we had something, Lord. I thought he cared for me. Why, Lord? Why?*

———

Kate had decided Josh and Joe needed schooling and had ordered some books and slates along with a box of chalk, which were delivered with the stove. School would be held at the cabin every day after morning chores and the baby's bath. The first day, she excitedly stood on the porch and rang a cowbell, announcing the start of school. First came Joe, trailed by Josh, both sweaty from stacking wood, and to her astonishment, Wounded Eagle followed right behind them.

———

Everyone had gathered in Max and Kate's yard for Sunday dinner. Millie and Kate had spread the feast on a quilt-covered flatbed wagon, and they all sat on hay bales. After the meal and before the pies were set out, Max asked the menfolk to meet him around back for a powwow. As they headed that way, he looked over his shoulder, hollering at the boys, "Joshua and Joseph!" The boys scrambled to their feet. "You two have been working like men all summer," he quietly said. "You need to be part of this."

Max and Henry sat on the back porch, and Freddy and Will sat on a fallen log. Wounded Eagle sat on the ground with Josh and Joey on either side. Henry believed that Wounded Eagle wanted to ask Jesus into his heart but couldn't understand clearly enough to be sure. That's why the powwow. Between Josh and Joe and Kate's school, Wounded Eagle had learned many words in English.

Max spoke first. "Wounded Eagle, what do you believe about Jesus?"

The Indian stood. He raised his arms and looked into the cloudless sky. "Beeg God so much love beeg world, He gave His One Son, hang on beeg cross, that who believe will not die but have living forever. John 3:16." Wounded Eagle then placed a fist over his heart, tears streaking the dust on his face. "Wounded Eagle have Jesus!"

The women out front heard whoopees, hallelujahs, and laughter coming from behind the house. In a water tank near the barn, that evening, there would be a baptism. It was decided and agreed by Wounded Eagle that his name would be changed. After that night, he would be called Samuel Weaver.

Kate served the pie while Millie rocked the baby. Little Jake was like medicine to her soul, helping to fill the empty places and easing the heartache. She looked out from the porch, smiling at the collection of people that had become her family. She loved them all and was even growing fond of Ada, Pearl, and Liz as they settled into life on the Western frontier. They were learning to cook and stitch, and were joining with the others in evening Bible study. There was so much to be thankful for.

She had asked Wounded Eagle once if he planned to go back to his people. He had placed a hand on each of the boys' blond heads and with a huge smile said, "These my people."

Someone noticed dust rolling in the distance, and then they heard the sounds of a wagon out front of the inn. No stage was due that evening. "I'll go check," Max called, grinning as he leaped "Wounded Eagle style" onto his horse and rode bareback through the field.

A covered wagon had pulled up in front of the inn; the dust still stirring. A big man came from behind it and tied his horse to the hitching post. "Silas? Is that you?" Max asked.

Then another man appeared, who Silas introduced as Pierre Montague. "And please meet my wife, Simone," Pierre said with a deep French accent. Simone was Indian, and after greeting Max, she began handing down the children who had been peering out from behind the wagon bench. Pierre proudly introduced his three boys, saying first their French name and then their Indian name. The two older boys were very polite and shook hands with Max. The little one, a toddler barely walking, just stared at him with huge brown eyes.

Pierre called up to the wagon, "Daughters, come meet Monsieur Reed." A girl of about fourteen, Max guessed, stepped out, her dark hair braided, her brown eyes flashing as she smiled a greeting to Max. She looked just like her mother. "This is Margot, or Laughing Waters. She is always happy." Margot shyly giggled. From behind her came the last of his five children. "Please meet my daughter, Maria. Her Indian name is Pale Moon."

Silas watched Max intently as he struggled to speak. He was stunned. Maria was tall and her hair was pale blond, almost like spun gold. Her skin, though tanned from the sun, was that of a white woman. She wore a deer-hide dress and beaded headband, and her hair was braided like Margot's. But she was, without a doubt, not Indian. Her eyes were wide, a deep sparkling blue. *Familiar,* Max thought. *Millie's eyes!* Then he stammered, "I'm—I'm very pleased to meet you all." And then to himself, *Lord God! You truly are a big God! Will wonders never cease.*

84

Part Two

AMAZING GRACE

"We do not weave the web of life; we are merely a strand in it.
Whatever we do to the web, we do to ourselves."
Chief Seattle

Chapter 16

There was no mistake; it was Silas was walking with purpose through the field between Millie's Inn and Max and Kate's cabin. *Oh dear Lord! I didn't think I'd ever see him again,* Millie thought. She stood on the porch where she had been rocking little Jake, and handed the baby off to Kate. She gathered her skirts and headed toward him, worry creasing her brow. They both picked up speed, each unsure of the other's state of mind.

Without hesitation, Silas pulled her into his strong arms. When she tried to speak, a sob escaped her throat, only to be followed by another. He said, "Let's take a walk, Millie."

She took the hand he offered, and he led her away from everyone's curiosity. They walked a way, not speaking. Silas didn't know where to begin. He never was good with words. Despite all the rehearsing he'd done, he suddenly blurted it out, "Darlin', I think I found your girl. I found Grace."

Millie stopped then turned toward him, her hands covering her heart. "Gracie? You found Gracie? Oh dear God! Silas, don't get my hopes up. We don't know if she's dead or alive. How can you make such a strong declaration? Don't do this to me." She pounded his chest, sobbing.

He hated seeing her like that. "It's a long story, Millie."

Glaring at him, she backed away. "Where did you supposedly find her? And where is she now, Silas?"

He looked down at his boots, hurting for her. *Lord, help me, Jesus.* "Millie, honey." He took a deep breath. "She's waiting in the dining room right now. She's in there with her—uh—family."

———

Simone was the only mother Pale Moon had ever known, and they loved each other deeply. When the child turned six summers, she had been marked for death by the chief of their tribe. She was condemned for bringing bad luck to their hunting grounds, which was depleted of game because "her people," the white emigrants, had pilfered the land.

Simone, then known as Sage Blossom, had been given the duty of caring for the little pale one when Indian warriors had returned with her long ago. The young Indian brave bound to marry Sage Blossom came to her in the night and warned that she must take the girl and run. He had even packed a pouch of supplies, and helped the two get beyond their village.

They were on the run for months, hiding at times in caves and hollow logs, hungry and cold in deep winter snows, sweltering in desert heat, and all but giving up in driving sandstorms. But Sage Blossom had prayed to the Mighty One and believed He would deliver them. And that He did. They heard it before seeing it: flowing swiftly in a canyon below, a cold stream - full of fish. It was there on the bank that Pierre Montague spotted them, dripping wet, splashing each other and laughing. It was an extraordinary sight, a lovely dark Indian woman and a very pretty white child. A small fire crackled on the beach, and fish bones were scattered about, evidence they'd been feasting on trout. When he called out to them, they clung to each other, terrified.

Pierre hesitated to come closer. From across the stream, he spoke calm, caring words, some in English and some in French. They understood neither, but from his kind demeanor, Simone began to feel confident, and they eventually went along with him as he led his horse and pack mules.

A trapper, Pierre had been gathering beaver pelts and working his way back home when he came across Sage Blossom and Pale Moon. He felt much compassion toward them, as it was obvious from their calloused and bleeding feet, their scrawny forms, with collarbones jutting out from beneath their tunics, that they had been on the run. The fish, no doubt, had been their first meal in a very long time.

Pierre was an independent trapper, very successful and well known among important fur-trading companies. He was respected by businessmen, emigrants, Indians, and mountain men. He lived alone in the finest log house Sage Blossom and Pale Moon had ever seen—the only one they'd ever been inside. He showed them to a separate room with a large bed, but for the first six months of staying in Pierre's house, they chose to sleep on the floor.

Pierre came and went, making sure they had ample food and supplies. He taught them how to build a fire in the stove and how to cook on it. Between his travels, Pierre tutored Sage Blossom and Pale Moon in English and French, and he taught them how to fry bacon and eggs. In no time, they were singing French folk tunes as they made moccasins and such from soft buckskin and beaver pelts Pierre gave them. Sage Blossom and little Pale Moon smoked fish they caught each day from the river behind Pierre's pasture, the very one where he had found them.

One warm spring day, Pierre announced they would take a two-day journey to purchase supplies at a French colony up north. "We will hitch up the larger wagon," he said. "I want to buy more chickens and perhaps a milk cow." He continued with his list of purchases, which included fabric and notions, so Sage Blossom and Pale Moon may learn to sew.

On the road, the three sat on the wagon seat, practicing their English and French and laughing joyfully. The ride was long, dusty, and bumpy, but with the two young women, Pierre decided it was most pleasant. The conversation turned to things of God, and Pierre said they would be going to church at the French village on Sunday. "In fact," he continued, looking straight ahead, "if you are agreeable, Sage Flower, we could be married at the same time."

She looked up at him, her dark eyes huge. "Ahh-greeb-el?"

Pierre returned her gaze lovingly. "Will—you—be—my—wife?"

Sage Blossom broke into a huge smile. "Oui, Monsieur Pierre."

As if interpreting, Pale Moon said in very fine English, "She said *yes!*" And the three burst into happy laughter.

———

Millie was praying and preparing herself mentally as she splashed water on her face and combed her hair. She pulled it back into a neat twist then paused at her reflection in Kate's mirror. The little lines around her eyes seemed more pronounced; her blond hair was streaked with gray. *God has brought you this far, Millie Thatcher. He won't let you down now.*

Before she was caught talking to herself, she hurried out to the porch, where Max and Kate waited with Josh, Joey, and baby Jake to walk with her to the inn. She didn't want to keep her guests waiting any longer. She had decided that was how she would welcome them: just like regular guests, the way she welcomed everyone. She vowed that she would not cry, and she would not single out Grace—if it was indeed Grace. She would just be herself. And she would not call her Grace, but Maria, as Max had advised.

Millie took a deep breath and pushed through the kitchen door and into the dining room, the Reed family right behind her. All resolve disappeared at the sight of the stunningly beautiful girl, standing tall, her sparkling blue eyes huge. It was like no one else was in the room. Millie walked to her daughter, a younger version of herself, and burst into tears. "Oh, Grace!" Then she pulled her into her arms and held her like she would never let go.

Chapter 17

The Montague family settled into three suites and all pitched in to help around the place. The two older boys, Andre and Louis, were adept at stacking wood, and as they helped Josh and Joey, a friendship developed. "Wanta see our fort?" Joey offered one afternoon, when work was done.

The two dark-haired brothers said in unison, "Oui!" Josh and Joey looked at each other, shrugged, and they all raced to the barn.

Later Pierre set out to look for them and heard laughter coming from that direction. He quietly slipped inside the barn door, staying in the shadows to observe his boys at play with the Reed twins. "C'mon, Louie. You can do it," Josh called. "Here, I'll show ya." The boys had rigged a rope from the big beam in the rafters of the barn and tied a knot near the bottom. Never mind that it appeared to be Pierre's finest rope used for his pack animals. They were taking turns swinging out from the hayloft and landing in a huge pile of hay in the middle of the floor. Never mind that the hay had been moved there from nearby storage bins.

Louis finally got the courage to swing out, but came back to the safety of the loft each time, afraid to let go. Joey had the bright idea: he and Josh would stay below and catch him. "C'mon, Louie, you can do it. Andre will be up there to catch ya if you don't let go, and we'll both catch ya if ya do!" Pierre kept a hand over his mouth to keep from laughing out loud.

When Louis let go and the boys tried to catch him, the force of the boy knocked them both down. All three lay there in the hay, holding their sides, laughing. Andre hollered a big war cry—*Where did that come from?*—and swung out, landing on top of all three.

Pierre burst out laughing, giving himself away. "Excusez moi? Are you gentlemen having fun?"

Startled, they jumped to their feet. When they saw Pierre laughing, all four replied with a hearty "Yep!"

———

They had combed every inch of the place—the inn, the outbuildings, the Reed cabin, even the Montague's covered wagon. Grace was gone. Bible study was to take place that evening after supper. Millie had been sure Grace would be coming with Max and Kate, since she had helped with the baby during school that day. Kate figured she was with Millie. A sense of panic filled the room, with everyone talking at once then not speaking at all. Silas tried to console Millie.

Max stepped up and took charge. "We need to stay calm and organize a search." Realizing the sun was going down quickly, he sent Freddie and Will to gather the horses and get them saddled. As Max was pairing up the search parties, he realized Samuel was no longer in the room. By the time the men and boys headed out, Max reckoned Samuel was way ahead of them.

They agreed to return by dark and ride out again at daybreak if they hadn't found Grace. Kate rocked her baby and prayed. Margot attended her two little brothers. And Simone comforted Millie, saying, "She is strong and brave. She is a survivor. We must trust the Mighty One."

Henry first noticed Samuel's boots near the cot and then his work clothes heaped on top. The Indian garb that had hung on a peg was gone. So were his bow and arrows. So was Henry's Winchester. Following a hunch, the old man hobbled his way out back. *Sho nuff, he done took that half-broke colt.* But no one seemed to notice that the mare in Max's field was gone too.

Samuel rode all night, letting the horse have his head, knowing Grace was on the mare. In the early light of dawn, he finally spotted tracks and felt sure it was her.

The night he was baptized, he had become a new man. He was Samuel, a child of the King. He was redeemed, washed by the blood of the Lamb. But he was still Indian. With God's help, he would find the fair one, Pale Moon.

Millie was beside herself when the men returned with no sign of Grace. *Oh Lord, why would you bring her back, only to take her again? Please, God, please.*

Hardly anyone slept that night, keeping a vigil, hoping Grace would return on her own. Before dawn, the men road out again, Max with Josh and Joey heading north, Pierre and Andre going west the way they had come, Silas going east, and Will and Freddie, south. Each one was praying, searching for any sign of the missing girl. At the end of the long day, they returned empty-handed once again.

———

Something caught Samuel's eye. He backed his horse and bent to a low branch. A few strands of golden hair were snagged on a twig. He was on the right track, and he knew the country well. The deep woods would open onto acres of meadow before long. He would circumvent the field and climb onto high rocky ground, where he would have an expansive view. His intuition told him she would be making a beeline across the open area, back into the seclusion of the thick forest on the other side. He waited. According to the sun beginning its descent in the west, he guessed it was midafternoon.

Samuel began to wonder if he'd been wrong, when suddenly she burst on the scene, galloping the Palomino hard, like a streak of platinum, her long hair and the mare's tail flying wildly. Instead of the woods, she headed toward a narrow break in the rock wall. She knew the country too.

Samuel scanned the area, calculating the quickest way to get down that canyon ahead of her. Suddenly, out of the corner of his eye, he saw movement across the opening she was headed for. A cat—a big one, well camouflaged; the color of the rocky crags it crouched upon. Grace was nearly at the entrance. Samuel raised Henry's rifle, praying.

It sounded like a canon exploding, but it killed the wild cat. Its limp body tumbled into the canyon below. Grace's horse, terrified, reared and threw her to the ground. Samuel's relief that he'd killed the cat turned into a sickening feeling that he might have caused something dreadful to happen to Pale Moon. He raced down the side of the rocky outcropping without caution, loose rocks spewing in all directions. As he jumped off his horse and ran to her, she raised her head, groggy and disoriented. He knelt by her side and helped her slowly sit up. Her face was scraped, bloody, and covered with dirt. Her hair was tangled with pieces of twig. *She's the most beautiful woman I've ever seen,* Samuel thought.

"Ohhh, my ankle," she groaned.

"Can you stand?" Samuel asked tenderly.

"Thirsty. So thirsty."

He scooped her up before she could protest and carried her, running, into the canyon to water. Though she was nearly as tall as he, she was light as a feather. The mountain stream was icy cold. He sat her gently against the trunk of a big pine and filled the canteen that had been strapped over her shoulder. She guzzled it down, letting water run down her chin onto her tunic. He tore thick moss from the bank, soaked it in the water, and packed it around her swelling ankle. As her fogginess began to lift, she realized this

Indian, who spoke English, who treated her with such kindness, was Samuel.

Once more the searchers returned in darkness the following night. No Grace. They were worn out, dehydrated, and aching, but they determined to go again in the morning, changing their course a bit. They would leave Josh and Joey home with Kate. The boys had been real troupers, and they wanted so badly to find Grace, but it was just too much for ten-year-olds.

Chapter 18

In the mist of dawn, the next day, Simone thought she heard something. She had been up before daybreak, pacing out front of the inn, praying, waiting. She braced herself in anticipation. It sounded like someone was coming from the west. She knew the men had not yet gone out. Could it be Pale Moon? She listened intently, realizing it was more than one horse, walking slowly. A silhouette came into view: two riders on one pony, leading a horse. *It is her!* She fell to her knees. *Thank you, Mighty God, thank you.* Simone moved to receive them, trying to convey assurance.

Samuel slipped from the horse and gently lifted Pale Moon. He carried her limp form toward the building. "She is well, Sage Blossom, one foot injured. Very tired," he said.

As they entered through the front door, Max and Silas came through the back to get coffee Millie had just brewed. At the sound out front, Millie turned from the stove and burst through the kitchen door, but she stopped short when she recognized her daughter. She was determined not to overreact this time and to let the exhausted child sleep. She wrapped her arms around Simone, both women softly crying. "Our prayers have been answered, Simone." Then, arm in arm, the two mothers headed upstairs, Millie instructing Samuel to follow. "Let's take her to her room."

But instead of stopping at the suite Grace shared with Margot, Millie continued to the end of the long hallway and unlocked the exquisite chamber prepared for Grace so long ago. She turned back the feather comforter. "Lay her here, please, Samuel." When he had done so, Millie suddenly grasped the reality that Samuel had found her. He looked exhausted. "Samuel!" She pulled him into a strong hug. "Thank you, dear one. You rode out before we even knew it. You were so determined. You are very, very brave. Thank you, Sam, for bringing our girl home."

Grace was too weak to be aware of her surroundings. She woke the next day when sunrise shone through lace curtains, casting light on the wedding picture. Her breath caught at the recognition. Slowly she sat up, taking in her surroundings. *Where am I?* Her eyes scanned the heavenly place, the lovely furnishings, and a soft glow of warmth from the wood stove. Her eyes moved to the pitcher and basin, and then, almost missing it, to the initial G embroidered on a linen towel. *Has this room been prepared for me?* Again she looked at the wedding picture. There was no denying; it had to be her mother and father.

Grace slid back beneath the downy quilt, wincing at the pain in her ankle. She felt so weary, but she lay there awake, her blue eyes staring at the ceiling, tears dampening her white feather pillow.

With two mother's tending her, Grace gained strength and slowly came back to life. Silas had fashioned a crutch to help take the weight off her ankle, and in a few days she was getting around pretty well. When Kate walked in one afternoon with the baby, Grace lit up. "Would you want to rock him to sleep for me?" Kate asked sweetly, picking up right where they'd left off before Grace ran away. She knew they would talk in time, but for then she just wanted Gracie to feel needed and loved.

Grace hugged Jake close, the feel of him and the sweet smell of his hair a healing balm to her soul. He smiled up at her, his chubby fingers touching her chin. She couldn't help hug him tighter, smiling back. She thought of the wedding picture on the wall of her heavenly room. *The young couple is so happy. My mother and father.*

The happiness they must have shared when God blessed them with a baby. With me. She couldn't imagine someone taking little Jake. *Oh dear God, it must have been terrifying for Millie. For my mother—ma mere.*

She realized how foolish it was to run away. She had felt so bewildered. Samuel had understood, quietly listening to her ranting that night as they sat by the stream. He had searched for her, cared for her, saved her from a wild cat. He had built a fire on the beach and speared fish and cooked them for her. He had found wild berries and picked them for her. Mostly, he had listened to her. He was understanding and compassionate.

She couldn't cope with having to choose between two mothers, with having to leave one family for another. She cried and carried on. Samuel had just listened. Tenderly he wiped away her tears until the next round of sobbing. Then he calmed her again, brushing her hair back and listening. Sometime late in the night, he finally spoke. He looked at her with empathy and then broke into a smile. In the firelight, his long black hair tied back, Grace knew there was something about him—a gentle strength, a kind of joy.

"Pale Moon, do you not see? You are favored!" he said, laughing.

Stunned by his comment, she asked, "Whose favor?"

"The Mighty One's. You have *two* mothers! I am twenty-three summers and have none. No mother, no father in all my years. I was Lone Wolf. No family until now." His smile widened. "Until Silas shot me and then matching boys brought me home."

Her eyes grew wide. "Silas shot you?"

He laughed, pointing at the scar on his shoulder. Then, in his halting English, he told her the whole story: How Silas had held up the stage and kidnapped Kate. How he had repented and turned to the Lord. He shared with her the funny way Kate and Max met; how she fell from the sky. And the strange "coincidence" that Silas became lost in blinding snow and stumbled upon the cabin of Pierre Montague. And How Millie had told Silas about her lost child. Samuel had Grace smiling and weeping throughout the night.

"You see, Pale Moon, the Mighty One weaves a blanket. A beautiful blanket! It is many colors, every thread a story. We are together not by mistake, but part of His great blanket."

A single tear escaped and dropped on Jake's cheek. Grace studied his perfectness: dark lashes, tiny fingernails, sweet rosebud lips. She loved him. If anything ever happened to Kate, she would love and protect him like her own. She tipped her head back, closing her eyes. *Simone was that to me. Simone loved me and protected me like I was her own. She saved my life. Simone. Sage Flower. Ma mere.*

———

Kate wasn't concerned that the schoolbooks had not yet arrived. Each day after sums, spelling, and reading from the Bible and Millie's mail order catalog, she gave the boys assignments from the resources that surrounded them. She had sent them out to catch frogs and then to report about the creatures' habitat, the things they ate, and so on. Josh, Joey, Andre, and Louie, with jars in tow, headed to the fishing hole riding double on two horses. Of course, the boys loved this part of school. Last time it was butterflies, but all except Louie were more partial to frogs. They had seen some huge frogs down there, but Kate didn't hand out very big jars.

As the boys approached the riverbank, they heard laughter and stopped short. It sounded like a girl laughing. They tied the horses and, like four little Indians, crept in for a closer look. Josh and Joey simultaneously clamped a hand over their mouths when they spotted Ada. In the water. With Will. They were about shoulder deep, splashing each other, giggling. The boys all looked at each other, silently trying to figure what they should do. Then, right before God and their four sets of eyes, Will kissed Ada.

"That was a big one," Joey whispered. The four boys got the giggles themselves and decided they'd better skedaddle. The next morning, they couldn't wait for the cowbell to ring.

"Before we start spelling," Kate began, "I'm anxious to know. Did you catch anything at the fishin' hole?"

"Oh, we caught somethin' all right," Josh said. "We caught Ada and Will kissin'!"

Kate gasped then choked, trying to take the news calmly. Then she realized Max was standing in the doorway. He took off his hat and scratched his head, trying his best not to burst out laughing. "Now *that's* a wonder."

Kate decided to forget about the frogs and came up with a new assignment. The boys would conduct interviews. After she explained the process, they picked Henry for the first one.

Chapter 19

It was a lesson indeed. Henry had been born into a slave family that picked cotton for rich white folks on a big plantation in the South. "Of course us colored folks dinna live in no big house, no sah. All us seven chilluns an' mammy an pappy—even granny—live in a shack out by da cotton fields. We dinna have no schoolin', no sah. Hardly nuff t'eat. But on the Lawd's Day afta pickin', we all gatha at a big field out ina woods." Henry chuckled at the memory. "An we sing them ol Negra spirituals to the Lawd."

Henry had softened the harshness of it for the sake of the young ones, but when he got to the part about his wife and son, he choked up. "The slave tradahs come through one day, pullin' a big wagon. My boy, Thomas, he only nine years ol'. They take him. Jest like that. Weren't nuthin' I could do but watch him go off in that big wagon." What he didn't tell was that his boy was wrenched from his arms, and Henry was lashed over and over for trying to follow. What he also didn't tell was that his pregnant wife witnessed it all and was also lashed for screaming frantically after her son. She lost the baby and then her life. In two days, Henry had lost all he loved.

"But Thomas, he know the Lawd. And my Maybelle too. Someday we all be in heaven. Lawdy, Lawdy, what a day that will be! Me and mah family be dancin' a jig. Sho nuff." Henry chuckled. "Sho nuff."

Later that night, when the boys were getting ready to turn in, Joey said, "Hey, Josh? You think someday we'll be dancin' a jig with Mama? In heaven, I mean?"

Josh chuckled, "Sho nuff, Joe. Sho nuff." Then they hugged the kind of hug men give, with a hearty slap on the back. The two fell asleep with a smile on their dirty faces.

———

Interviews were just about as good as catching frogs, the boys decided. So they asked Kate if they could interview Millie. "Well, that's a fine idea," she replied. Since Millie was so busy all the time, at Kate's suggestion, they would ask just one question of her. It was Kate's thought to keep it light.

A few days later, the interview took place in the kitchen. The four boys pulled up a chair at the small kitchen table, while Millie worked dough on the counter with her hands. Andre began. "Miss Millie, we just have one question for today. How did you meet Dallas Thatcher?"

Millie stopped kneading and broke into a huge smile, her deep-blue eyes turning even bluer. She looked like a young girl again, with a smudge of flour on her cheek. "I'll never forget that day. It was at a barn raisin' back in Oklahoma. Ranchers and farmers for miles around gathered at the Jacobson place. The women prepared food for days. Papa hitched up the wagon at daybreak, and him and Mama, my brothers, and me loaded up the back with baskets of corn, breads and pies, corned beef, and jars of pickles. More stuff than that even, if I could remember. Dallas, he had just got work out at Calhouns, a big ranch on the other side."

She was back to kneading her dough, lost in the recollections. "The men were workin' hard all day, and I didn't notice him until we had the dinner spread, ready to eat. He walked right up to me—" She laughed. "He said, 'Does that happen to be a buttermilk pie, ma'am?' I said, 'Why yes, it is, I baked it fresh last night.' He said,

'Well, if that don't beat all. The purtiest girl in all of Oklahoma can make a buttermilk pie!'"

Millie blinked back to the present, remembering the boys sitting there. "How 'bout some cookies and milk? Well, *almost* cookies." She poured four cups of frothy milk and scooped four spoonfuls of cookie dough, since there was no space in the oven yet to bake them. The four thanked her with big smiles on their faces.

"Anyway, where was I? Oh yes, so Dallas ate two pieces of my pie *before* the meal and another after. The barn was nowhere finished, but some of the boys had fiddles, and Jack Calhoun had brought his guitar. Before long we were having a regular barn dance in the middle of the unfinished barn. Dallas asked me to dance every single dance, and I could tell the other girls were fumin' mad. After all, he was about the best lookin' cowboy any of us had laid eyes on. He ask my pa that very night if he could court me, and he found work at the ranch next to ours." She went on to tell them all the wonderful things about the handsome Dallas Thatcher and how they married two months into their courtship.

Millie pulled a roast out of the oven, added wood to the stove, and slid the pans of cookies in. Then she poured herself a cup of coffee and sat down with the boys. "Now then, you fellers have any questions?"

They had two. Joey asked, "What exactly is a barn raisin'?"

And little Louie asked, "Can you make us a buttermilk pie?"

She laughed and scooted her chair closer in. "I'm gonna let you four in on a little secret! Promise not to tell?"

"We promise," they blurted out in unison, shooting looks at each other at the excitement of it.

"First I'll explain that a barn raisin' is when a community of people gathers to help one family build a barn. It's too big a job, so everybody pitches in to help each other. Now, don't tell, but next week after the program, I'm gonna be makin' a big important announcement." She looked at each one. "Ready?"

The boys were chomping at the bit that they were the only ones in on Millie's announcement. "Yep!" they all said. Josh added, "And we promise not ta tell!"

Millie pulled in even closer and spoke just above a whisper. "We're gonna have a kind of barn raisin' right next door. Only instead of a barn it's gonna be a church raisin'!" Four sets of eyes grew big. "That's right," Millie continued. "We're gonna build us a church. Oh, and Louie, that might be a fine evenin' to serve buttermilk pie. Now don't y'all tell."

———

Kate insisted Josh and Joey wear their white shirts, even if the buttons were now a bit tight and the sleeves four inches short. They had been excited about the school program but now that it was time, it didn't seem like such a good idea. Even though the audience would be made up of family and friends, they were a bit nervous. "It's just like goin' to Bible study night," Max offered, hoping to encourage them. That and the anticipation of Millie's announcement, not to mention the buttermilk pie, rallied their courage.

Kate stood and handed Jake over to Max. Then she took the floor to make introductions. "First I want to say I am so very proud of my students, Andre, Louis, Josh, Joe, and Samuel. Well, Samuel is part time, learning English. All have been diligent in their sums and reading, mainly from the Bible. Even though we lack books on science and geography, these boys have learned firsthand from our surroundings, right here."

Jake let out a squeal and reached toward Kate. "Ma-ma-ma-ma," he fussed. Max shushed him and set him up on his shoulders. Kate continued, "These boys have learned more from all of you than they ever could have from a book. You all have given your time and stories from the heart for their interviews." A chuckle spread through crowd. "Thank you all." She sniffed and decided she'd better get on with it.

Josh and Joey were up first, standing tall in their outgrown white shirts, faces clean, hair trimmed and combed neatly. They simultaneously cleared their throats, glanced at each other, and together said, "This Scripture is dedicated to Miss Kate." Then they recited Psalm 100 flawlessly.

> Make a joyful noise unto the Lord, all ye lands.
> Serve the Lord with gladness: come before His presence with singing.
> Know ye that the Lord He is God: It is He that hath made us, and not we ourselves;
> We are His people, and the sheep of His pasture. Enter His gates with thanksgiving, and into His courts with praise; be thankful unto Him, and bless His name.
> For the Lord is good; his mercy is everlasting; and His truth endureth to all generations.

Everyone clapped enthusiastically. Kate could be heard sniffling, and Max got choked up too.

Andre and Louis were next. They dedicated their Scripture memorization to their parents. Together they also recited Psalm 100, but to their father's delight, in French. Pierre chuckled and Simone wiped a tear. Again the crowd clapped heartily, smiling and nudging one another.

Samuel came to the front then, and with a big smile said, "Thees one deda—" He glanced down at Josh and Joe sitting on the rug in front of him.

They whispered, "Dedicated."

"Dedah. Thees one dedah—" He looked up at the audience, directly at Grace. "Thees one—for Pale Moon. Psalm 23."

> The Lord is my shepherd; I shall not want. He maketh me to lie down in green pastures; He

105

leadeth me beside still waters. He restoreth my soul:
He leadeth me in the paths of righteousness for his
name's sake.

Grace hung on every word as Samuel recited to her, as if no
one else was in the room. They were both remembering the green
pasture, the still waters—the day Samuel found her, rescued her, and
helped her turn to the Lord. *Yes, Lord, you restoreth my soul.*

Chapter 20

Kate and Max hadn't had time in ages, it seemed, to sit on the porch in the evening, sipping coffee, talking. Baby Jake was down for the night, and Josh and Joey were camping out behind the cabin with Andre and Louis. Johnny Boy didn't have the spunk anymore to keep up with the boys. He just lay sleeping on the porch next to Kate and Max. The day had been a hot one, but was cooling, tall grasses bending in the breeze.

"I'm so happy for Millie," Kate mused. "She and Grace are becoming closer all the time, and now, with the church raising and all, her prayers are surely being answered. And Silas—he's a pillar. They make a fine pair, don't ya think, Max?"

"Most assuredly they do. I'm still flabbergasted, though, at Ada and Will. No wonder she didn't go back east with her sisters."

"I never put it together," said Kate. "I know it's just temporary, to settle Papa's estate, but I would have expected Ada, of all three, to go. She always set her cap for a man of higher station; she loves the social scene."

Max chuckled. "And here she is head over heels for a drifter like Will."

From around the side of the house came Louie. "Will's from New York," he said with confidence. "His family owns a steamship line. They came over from Germany. His brother goes to lawyer school."

Max and Kate turned in their rockers, mouths open in astonishment. "Huh?" Max said, stupefied.

"How do you know all that, Louie?" Kate asked sweetly.

Louie shrugged. "I interbewed him."

———

After Millie's announcement, the place was abuzz with energy. Everyone was filled with new purpose, excited about the church raising. Since it had gotten late, they unanimously decided to go ahead with the buttermilk pie and schedule another meeting Friday after supper. Max had sketched some plans, and the men agreed they would fell timbers from a thick stand up high then skid them down to the site once it snowed. They could get to work on that right away.

They talked excitedly about everyone having a part, a job to do. Millie shared her vision for the interior, which would feature a big cross behind the pulpit.

Joey excitedly raised his hand.

"Yes, Joe?" Millie asked.

"Me and Josh could whittle it for ya."

Josh looked doubtful. He whispered in Joey's ear, "She means a *big* one, Joe, not a whittled one."

"I'm *talkin'* about a big one. We can do it, Josh! Sam can help us."

Millie replied, "That's a fine idea, boys. Somebody write that down. Joshua and Joseph Reed are in charge of the cross. And Sam too." All three beamed.

Silas stood and cleared his throat. "I wanta bring up somethin' real important to Miss Millie. The winders. Us men can do the heavy work on the buildin' right up to the steeple. But the winders have ta be ordered from some outfit back east. And I reckon they ain't cheap. Millie and I talked about it some, and she's hopin' we can get the money together for glass winders. Now here's an idear I been thinkin' on. Ta raise the money for winders, what do y'all think of puttin' our talents together, especially the women, to make stuff for a trading post right in this here buildin'?"

Simone surprised everyone by raising her hand. "My daughters make beautiful moccasins."

Both Grace and Margot smiled shyly, and Margot said, "Ma mere does lovely beadwork."

"And I have pelts to contribute for many uses," offered Pierre.

Sam jumped up and ran out through the kitchen. He came back a couple minutes later with a rolled up elk hide. The boys helped hold it up for all to see. An amazing mural was painted on the tanned side. Samuel was smiling his big smile. "I make!"

Millie gasped at the beauty of it. "Oh, Samuel, you did this?"

Kate was taken aback too. "It's incredibly beautiful, Samuel."

Grace chimed in, "You are truly an artist." *And so much more,* she thought. *So much more.*

———

Travel came to a halt by mid-October, as winter arrived early, but it gave everyone the chance to get busy on their tasks for the trading post and church raising. Grace finished two sample pairs of tiny moccasins and gave one to her little brother, Tony, and the other to baby Jake. They were very soft doeskin, lined with fur. Kate couldn't quit smiling; so thankful her boy's little feet would be kept warm all winter. "Thank you, Grace. You are so kind." Kate drew her into a hug.

"And now I will get busy for the trading post," Grace declared, with newfound intention.

Henry didn't come to the meetings, because he wasn't feeling well; he seemed to be tired all the time. Nobody said it out loud, but they knew his time was near the end. Millie insisted she give him a room in the house, saying, "It's the least I could do for such a loyal friend." Henry had stuck by her since the beginning. Samuel carried the old man in through the kitchen, following Millie.

Grace was waiting at the foot of the stairs. "His room is ready," she said sweetly and led them straight to her own room, all soft and white.

"Grace," Millie began.

"I want him to have it. I wish to take care of him. It's my privilege," replied Grace.

Henry sank into the thick mattress, eyes closed but smiling. *Lawdy, Lawdy. Them young folks gots no idea. No suh. No idea. This the fust time ol' Henry ever been in a real bed. Sho nuff. Maybe ah's already gone ta heaven.*

Henry and Grace had hit it off from the first day she arrived. He was kind, gentle, and accepting. He convinced her that God had his hand on her life. "Weren't no acc'dent you bein' here," he said. "The good Lawd, He knows da plans He done gots for you, Gracie girl, sho nuf."

Most of the time, the old man slept, occasionally taking a sip of tea or broth brought by Millie. Grace pulled the rocker up close and read to him from the Bible, a suggestion from Samuel. "Henry—he read Good Book when I lay wounded. It very much comfort."

Henry watched Grace and Samuel, the way they looked at each other. Samuel couldn't take his eyes her, and Grace hung on every word Samuel spoke. Henry thought, *Ah's old and ah's tired, but ah ain't dead yet. No suh. Ah's still gots work ta do! Sho nuff.*

"He's a good'n, dat Samuel." Gracie jumped, startled when Henry spoke, thinking he was asleep. "He be strong an' he gots good sensibilities too. You cain't do no bettah, Gracie girl. No suh!"

Grace smiled, fumbling with the Bible on her lap. "Well, I do agree, Henry. He's a fine man." Henry had already fallen back to sleep, but she kept talking. "He's so caring and happy. I love his big smile, his big heart." She rested her head on the chair back and started talking to the ceiling. "He's so thankful for the smallest blessing. Like we all should be." Henry opened one eye, smiled, and closed it. "I do care for him," she continued, "very much." She closed her eyes, thinking of his handsome face, those dark eyes, and the way he made her feel pretty.

Three days later, with the family gathered at his side, Henry abruptly sat up, opened his eyes wide, and called out, "Ah's comin', Maybelle! Glory. Glory. Oh mah sweet Lawd!" His face was radiant. And then, just like that, Henry was gone. They buried him a few days later.

Two weeks following, they buried another loyal friend: Johnny Boy. He was as bad off as Henry had been, going blind and hardly able to get around anymore. The boys carved a fine cross for him and pounded it in the ground right in line: Clayton Alexander, Henry Weaver, John the Baptist. The graveside service was a solemn affair—until Max whispered something to Kate that got her tickled. Clasping a hand over her mouth did no good, for neither she nor Max could hold it in. They laughed out loud.

"What's so funny, Max?" Josh said, scowling.

"Yeah, Max, what's so funny?" repeated Joey.

Max got himself together and cleared his throat. "I'm sorry, boys. It's not funny. But can you imagine a hundred years from now when travelers stop by to read these markers? They're gonna be downright dumbfounded to find John the Baptist buried right here on the Western frontier."

Chapter 21

Christmas Day delivered two feet of snow, to everyone's delight. All production had come to a stop as the women prepared a bountiful dinner in celebration of the birth of Jesus. Small gifts were exchanged; mostly items they were making for the trading post. Simone had crafted leather headbands beaded in brilliant colors for each of the boys: Andre, Louie, little Tony, Josh, Joey, and baby Jake. All six wore them proudly, right through dinner.

The past few months of working together had bonded them into a tight-knit family. The women stitched and wove and beaded and quilted and laughed every afternoon, stopping only to prepare a meal or when Millie insisted they bundle up and go for a walk. The men laid a foundation for the church building, and right on time, the first snows allowed them to skid big timbers to the building site as planned.

In March, Max and Silas built a counter, shelves, and sign for the Thatcher Inn Trading Post, and everyone busied themselves cleaning, waxing, and preparing for the incoming travelers. In mid-April, the supply wagon pulled in, loaded with Millie's order. The following week, the first Wells Fargo coach of the season arrived. Kate hadn't heard from Liz and Pearl, and she couldn't wait for their arrival. It's not that she missed them so much, but if they had indeed received her letter, their arrival would be a cause for celebration.

Just before Jake's birthday in May, a covered wagon pulled up, and to everyone's surprise, Kate's sisters were in it. They couldn't resist a little complaining, the grime of the trail and all, but when everyone gathered after supper, they were like schoolgirls, full of excitement.

"Well, to start off," began Pearl, "we did get Papa's estate settled, and we were able to lease the ranch to good people."

Liz cut her off. "And you ladies will be so excited. We brought back Mama's sewing machine. And not only that, we brought Lucy! She's about ready to deliver a litter too." The sisters went on and on about this and that, including listing every item loaded in the wagon.

Kate elbowed Max and whispered, "What if they didn't get the letter?"

He put his arm around her shoulder. "Be patient, sweetheart." Liz and Pearl continued on until Kate was ready to burst. She realized then that the girls were looking straight at her, nodding.

"Go ahead, Kate, tell 'em what else."

"Well, uh. Just a minute." Kate hurried over to where Liz and Pearl were standing in front of the hearth. The three seemed to be having a conference. Max said a quick prayer, and everyone wondered what was going on. Then Kate turned to face her family. "Liz and Pearl asked me to share somethin' special." When she looked at Millie, Kate was suddenly filled with emotion. With a shaky voice, she blurted out, "They brought windows!" The crowd gasped. Kate started bawling, and Max was at her side in three strides.

Liz stepped up. "The windows for the new church are a contribution from the estate of Clayton Alexander, our papa." Millie burst into tears of her own, and Silas hugged her close. "Ya hear that, darlin'? The church is gonna have glass winders."

Kate gathered herself. "Nothing would make Papa happier, Millie. You were so kind and gracious to him. It's the least we can do."

Early the next morning, with great exuberance, the men were unloading the wagon, carefully storing the windows that had been packed in straw. Max was first to notice riders heading their way—three of them, riding hard. It was a US marshal and two deputies. They stopped their work, and Max took the lead. "Mornin', Marshal. What can we do for ya?"

"We're looking for a Silas Mitchell." Silas stepped out, took off his hat, and raked his fingers through his hair.

"That'd be me," Silas stated, his chest tightening.

The marshal dismounted from his horse. "Silas Mitchell? You're under arrest for theft of US Government documents."

During the day, Millie was strong for everyone else, but that night she wept and prayed and lashed out at God. *Why, Lord? Why can't I ever keep the ones I love? It was Silas's boss that was the culprit. Silas returned every stolen item he could find. He's turned his life over to you, Lord. He loves you. Ya gotta help him outa this mess. Please, God.*

———

Max, Pierre, Samuel, Will, and Freddie had a powwow. "It won't be easy," Max began. "In fact, it's maybe impossible, but for Silas, we gotta try. You all with me?"

"Me with you," stated Samuel.

"Oui," said Pierre.

Will didn't hesitate. "You bet, Max."

And Freddie said, "I'm in."

Before the marshal hauled Silas off, he and his deputies gave in to Kate's call for breakfast. This gave Silas a chance to speak with Millie and also to mull over the missing tinderbox the marshal had charged him with stealing. "There *weren't* no tinderbox on that stage. I cain't figure it out," he said to Max. "Boss said back when we took Miss Kate hostage—Lord forgive me—that exact stage was s'posed ta have a treasure box full a gold certificates. But there weren't none."

The marshal countered, "Oh, there was definitely a box. Maybe concealed, but that coach was carrying a tinderbox all right. Unless you confess the whereabouts of it, we have no choice, Mr. Mitchell, but to take you in."

The word *concealed* got Silas thinking. Just before the marshal's deputies escorted him out to the horses, he pulled Max aside and described where he had forced the Wells Fargo stagecoach over the edge of a cliff, into the deep canyon. Max patted Silas on the back. "You're a good man, Silas. We will be prayin'."

———

Kate tried to talk Max out of going to find the box. "Max," she pleaded, "surely the others can find that place Silas described. We need a man to stay behind, to protect us women."

"Well, honey, ya got the boys and your dog's here now. You all stay together at the inn; you'll be safe. We'll leave you plenty ammunition."

She jutted out her chin. "Well, if ya don't care about me," she pouted, "what about the baby?"

Max wrapped his arms around her. "Katy, darlin', you know I love you and my family more than life itself. But don't ya want to help free Silas? And honey, Jake's over a year old. Isn't it about time ta stop callin' him *the baby*?" He looked at her and smiled—the smile with the dimple.

"Max," she said shyly, looking up at him with big eyes, "I'm not *talkin'* about Jake."

It took a moment to sink in. "Are you sayin' what I think you're sayin'? Kate, are you—are we?" All she could do was nod, because she was doing that laughing-crying thing. Max scooped up his wife and twirled her around. "Wahoo!" he yelped. "I love you, Mrs. Reed."

Chapter 22

It took a few days to reach the place Silas had described. Pierre had offered to drive his small, sturdy wagon, since they would be passing the spot where Max's wagon had broken down, the very place God had dropped Kate into his lap. He hoped some of the things they'd stashed might still be there. Silas had also described the cave where Boss hid their loot and where Silas had heaved Kate's trunk deep into a chasm.

Samuel was in the lead, his horse prancing with energy, as if he knew they were on a great mission. They spotted the coach all right, far below, as Silas had described. It was a mass of splintered wood, like a broken toy. Max scratched his head. "It's impossible. No way down."

The men walked and rode their horses along the ridge, looking for any conceivable way to get to the canyon floor. Pierre observed, "If we could get to the other side somehow, there is a way. You see the switchbacks and that much more gentle slope. If we could only get to the other side." They rode on for a few more miles, pausing here and there to gauge the distance across. It did narrow some, but it was still a good twenty feet.

Max took off his hat and wiped a sleeve across his face. He was sweating, and it wasn't even hot. They were sitting in their saddles, trying to figure out what to do. He didn't notice that Samuel wasn't with them. Freddie, probably the quietest, suggested they pray.

At that very moment, less than a quarter mile ahead, came a chilling battle cry. Samuel was tearing full speed, coming out of nowhere toward the edge of the canyon. "Lord Jesus!" Max shouted, a look of terror his face—on all their faces. Sam's horse was airborne. It seemed horse and rider were suspended over that canyon for a lifetime. All of a sudden, he landed. Then he waved and smiled from ear to ear, safe on the other side.

While Samuel spent the rest of the day picking through shattered remains of the coach, Max and Pierre found Kate's trunk deep in the cave, just as Silas had explained. Thanks to Simone, Pierre's wagon contained items for survival: a drum of water, a pouch of jerky, a few tools, and a torch. Pierre smiled. "She's a very good woman, my Simone."

Freddie and Will kept an eye on Samuel like two watchmen on duty. All at once, Samuel's shouts echoed off the canyon walls. His exclamation wasn't clear, but he held something over his head, his face beaming, signifying victory

It was growing dark, and the men knew they would need to set up camp separate from Samuel. They also knew he would manage on his own just fine.

For a day and a half, they rode back toward home, trusting to meet up with Samuel, but the trail curved to the north, leaving any view of the canyon behind. They stopped at the place where it all started, where Max's wagon had broken down so long ago. Max chuckled. "Boy howdy, the Lord sure knew what he was doin'," he said, more or less to himself.

The men watered their horses and ate a bite, while Max investigated the cave for goods left behind. He was lost in memories: Kate landing in his lap, her berry cobbler, the way the boys took to her, trading Delilah to the Indians, Kate nursing his brothers back to health. *Katy. I love her so much, Lord. Thank you. Thank you. And for our babies, thank you so much.*

There was a commotion outside the cave. Max drew his pistol and then recognized the hearty laughter. "What taking you cowboys so long?" Samuel said, sitting on his horse, the tinderbox tied behind him. He had backtracked to find them after pulling up out of the canyon a dozen miles beyond.

———

After the men returned with the box, Millie composed a letter to go out on the next westbound stage, letting the marshal know. She had carefully crafted it, using veiled words, lest it fall into the wrong hands. The box would have to be safeguarded at the inn or somewhere on the grounds until delivery to the US government. It made her uneasy just thinking about it. Of course, it was locked up tight so none of them actually handled the gold certificates, but they'd be inviting trouble if it was found out.

The marshal had delivered Silas to federal court in San Francisco, which was near San Quentin Prison, where Silas would be setting up camp if convicted. In the meantime, he was kept in the county jail. *Well, Lord, I know ya have me here for some reason,* he prayed. *Help me do the right thing in all this. If I never get back to Millie and all the others, Lord, I thank ya from a humble heart for the time we had. Please watch over 'em, Lord Jesus.*

Days turned into weeks and weeks into months. No word from San Francisco reached Millie. Nothing. Work continued at a steady pace on the church, however Millie's heart wasn't in it. But she and Gracie had grown closer, daughter now sustaining mother. Unbeknownst to the others, it was Samuel who sustained Grace.

Every evening after supper, the family held a prayer vigil for Silas. Millie wrote again, addressing her letter this time to the "Honorable Federal Judge," whoever he might be. About three weeks later, a Pony Express rider raced to a halt out front to deliver a letter. The rider barely stopped then raced off in a whirlwind of dust.

Millie collapsed on the porch steps, ripping the envelope open. Evidently her first letter had never made it. The westbound stage that carried it had been hijacked and robbed. The letter implied that she could expect a visit from the US Marshal's office in mid-September, two weeks away.

Kate walked in the next morning after breakfast, Jake toddling along beside her. Even though it took twice as long to get around, she was grateful he was walking, as it was a relief with her bulging midsection. Millie was treadling away on the Singer sewing machine the girls had brought from home. "Mornin', Millie. It's good to see you busy on trading post projects again."

"Oh, this isn't for the tradin' post, honey," Millie replied. "It's for that new baby of ours." She sounded chipper again, like a woman with hope. "We are way behind makin' diapers and buntings and little pink dresses, I might add." Millie winked, a big smile on her face. She looked like her old self.

On September 17, a Wells Fargo stagecoach pulled up, shotgun messengers in front and back. The same marshal that had arrested Silas stepped out. Millie ushered him through the front door and back to the kitchen. "Is Silas all right, sir? This box we turn over to ya, is it his ticket to freedom? Has he been eatin' good?"

The marshal pulled out a chair from the kitchen table. "Now hold on, ma'am, first things first. Ya got any coffee on the stove?" Millie poured two cups and sat opposite him. At the same time, Max, Kate, Jake, Josh, and Joey entered through the back door, causing a ruckus.

When Max saw the law sitting at Millie's table, he simply said, "I'll go fetch it."

With the six of them watching, the marshal unlocked the box and sifted through the documents. Then he locked it again. Millie looked straight in the marshal's eyes and pleaded, "Well?"

"Here's the situation, ma'am. Upon the return of these documents, the government has agreed to grant leniency to Silas Mitchell, dropping all charges—under one condition."

"Go on, Marshal." Millie's face was flushed, a hanky twisted in her hands.

"Well, uh, maybe we should walk out to the coach." They all jumped up. Because of Kate's bulk, her chair fell over backward, clattering to the floor. The marshal hollered at his deputy, the stage door opened, and out stepped Silas.

"Silas!" Millie ran from the porch straight into his arms. "Oh, Silas. Nobody told me you were out here."

Silas choked up. "I missed ya so much, Millie girl. Y'all too." He nodded at Max's family while still holding tight to Millie.

Millie threw her arms around his neck and kissed him openly. "Silas, I figured you were still in jail!"

"Excuse me, ma'am," the marshal said. "We need to get something settled. As I mentioned, there's a condition to be met, before Silas gets off."

Trying to soften the blow, Silas said, "Yeah, well, they's droppin' all charges against me with one "stipulashun.""

The stage door swung open and out jumped the grimiest, filthiest child Millie had ever seen. "Hey! Where's the privy? I gotta take a—" Silas clamped his big hand over the boy's mouth just in time.

"Uh, this here is—uh, I'd like y'all ta meet my—uh, recent adopted, uh, son, Cody Walton—the stipulashun.

Chapter 23

Silas had missed out on so much. The church was mostly built, and it was a sight to behold. Everyone said, his idea for the trading post had been a big success.

Lucy had given birth to five pups. In June, when the pups were big enough, Kate made an assignment: her students would draw straws for the first pick. Four of the pups were nearly identical, miniatures of their mother and future cow dogs. Number five, the runt of the litter, was different. He was all brown, while the others were brown and white. One of his ears stuck up and the other down. He was smaller than the rest. Samuel, even though he had second pick, chose that one, the runt.

The Reed twins were set on giving their dogs biblical names out of regard for their father. The Montague boys thought it a good idea, and after a lengthy powwow, they had it settled: Peter, Andrew, James, and John. Louie called his pup Petie, Joey's was dubbed Andy, Joshua stuck with James, and Andre nicknamed his dog AJ for the apostle John, not to be confused with John the Baptist.

Silas was tickled to death over Max and Kate being blessed with another baby on the way. And to him, Millie was as beautiful as ever. During the time he was in that San Francisco jail, he had dreamed of them getting hitched, maybe the first wedding at the new church.

But now he had another responsibility—one that scared him more than anything he'd ever faced.

———

Silas had met Cody in jail. He couldn't believe the law would actually throw a thirteen-year-old in the pokey. The sad truth was that he had nowhere to go. He had been living on the streets, stealing to get by. His mother had run off with a gambling man, and his father, like so many others, was mining for gold and drunk most the time. Cody drank coffee and smoked Bull Durham—when he could steal it. He needed more than a haircut and bath, more than the rags he was wearing, more than shoes for his bare feet. Cody needed somebody to care.

Somehow, as their days behind bars slowly passed, Silas and Cody ended up watching each other's backs. They often sat on a filthy cot, sharing stories. "You remind me of *me* when I was a kid," Silas told the boy one evening. "A ornery, rebellious, thievin' little polecat."

"Are ya braggin' or complainin'?" Cody asked with a grin. They'd often go on like that, ribbing each other. But let any other inmate badmouth Silas, and Cody wouldn't stand for it. He didn't back down, even to the point of throwing a punch at a much bigger target. Silas grew very protective of the boy and silently prayed for him daily. *Lord, show me how to help this young man. I'm not the best example in the world, but I've walked in his bare feet. Show me, Lord.*

Silas knew from his own wasted youth where Cody was headed. The Lord convicted him to become the kind of father to Cody that he himself used to make-believe about.

Cody was given Henry's old cot in a bunkroom shared with Samuel. Right from the get-go, Samuel recognized the rebellious, stubborn, ornery hurt of the boy, but it didn't change his own cheerful outlook. Samuel spoke kindly, pointing out the features of Cody's new quarters. "Here is clean pillow and clean blanket for you. Over there is wash bucket, over there peg for britches." Since Cody didn't respond, Samuel casually picked up his pup and turned to go out the door.

"I don't need no half-breed tellin' me what ta do," Cody hollered at Samuel's back. Samuel stopped midstride and turned to face the boy, his face somber. Then just as quickly, he broke into a bright smile. "I no half-breed. Samuel all the way Indian!" He walked to where Cody sat on his cot, arms folded defiantly across his chest. "Here, you take care pup for me." He gently dropped the wagging puppy on Cody's lap, turned, and walked off to breakfast.

Later that week, Max stopped by home to check on Kate. He pushed open the door and froze on the spot. Kate was sound asleep, her head resting in her arms on the kitchen table. Jake was sprawled out on their bed, fast asleep as well. The dish tub on Kate's worktable was filled with dirty dishes, pots and pans piled high. Pieces of material were strewn across the floor. Max recognized them as from his mother's quilt. Chalk and slates were scattered on the table where Kate lay crumpled, evidence that school had taken place.

He kneeled next to her and peeked up, trying to see her face. "Katy? Honey?" he spoke just above a whisper. "Kate, are you all right, sweetheart?"

She lifted her head and looked at him groggily. Her eyes were puffy and red. Startling him, she abruptly stood. "No, Max! I'm not all right!" she yelled, scaring him half to death.

It had been her idea to enroll Cody in school, and he had stubbornly agreed under one "stipulashun": that the pup come too, right into the classroom. Even though dogs were not allowed, Kate had a talk with the other boys privately, and they agreed to it under the circumstances. They would leave their own puppies outside as previously settled.

Every day that week had been pure bedlam. Cody was disrespectful, talking back to Kate, refusing to do assignments. The other boys came to her defense, threatening to take him out back for a whipping. All the while Kate tried to remain calm and pleasant, with the puppy tearing up everything in site.

Little Jake was hot and cranky and let out a yelp whenever the rambunctious pup came near. The regular household chores piled up, for Kate was very weary. *Maybe if Samuel were here,* she had thought. But the men were pressed to finish the church roof before bad weather.

———

Cody became more and more attached to the dog. They did everything together. Late at night, with the pup snuggled up in Cody's bed, Samuel would hear the boy talking sweetly to it. "You're a good boy, puppy. Yes, you are. Now go to sleep. Awe, you're a smart one. Yes, you are. Good boy."

One morning, Samuel stood above boy and dog, both stretching awake. "Pup is yours now," he stated. "You take good care. I give to you."

Cody looked suspicious. "You mean for keeps?"

"Yes, for you."

A look came over Cody's face, a look that hadn't been seen in a long, long time. Something like a smile. He hugged the puppy close and looked up at Samuel. "Can I name him whatever I want?"

———

"Why don't ya name him a Bible name like all of ours?" Joey suggested thoughtfully.

"Yeah," the boys chimed in. "How 'bout Zacchaeus? He was a wee little man." They weren't really making fun of Cody's puppy being the runt. It just sounded like a good name.

"I ain't namin' him no sissy Bible name." He spit for emphasis, picked up his dog, and stormed off.

Lying in bed that night, Cody was mulling over all the possibilities for naming his dog. Then it hit him: the big sailor that landed in jail with him, back in Frisco. He was huge, with a great big chest and great big hands. Some called him Brute, but mostly they called him Goliath. That was it. Cody picked Goliath. No Bible name for his dog!

———

At the beginning of October, the men stopped church building long enough to split firewood—a mountain worth, it seemed to the boys. It was their job to stack it. Grace had offered to take over teaching duties, setting up in the dining room after breakfast each morning. Millie absolutely prohibited puppies, even Cody's. The trade-off was a sticky-bun break, right after reading and sums.

The first day, Silas stepped in to check on Cody; he was keeping a closer watch on the boy after he'd nearly sent Kate over the edge. His timing couldn't have been better; Millie was serving the boys milk and sticky buns right out of the oven. When she got to Cody with the milk pitcher, he said, "I'll have coffee."

Millie shot a look at Silas. He shrugged and said simply, "He takes it black."

During the wood stacking, Cody disappeared. It was late afternoon when Silas stopped by to check, and sure enough, Josh, Joey, and the Montague boys had at least two thirds of the woodpile stacked into neat rows. But Cody was nowhere in sight. "You fellers done good for today," Silas told them. "Y'all can take off."

"Aw, that's all right," said Josh. "We'll finish 'er up."

Silas replied, "Well, it's good of ya, but Cody's gonna do his share—just as soon as I find the little varmint."

Cody showed up for dinner. He sat off by himself with Goliath under his feet. Millie walked over to him, smiling sweetly, then got ahold of his arm and hefted him out of his chair. She marched him to the back porch, with the dog trotting happily behind. "You forgot to wash up, sweetheart. Hands and face—and the puppy stays out!"

Hmmm, she sure is strong for a woman, he thought.

Cody scarfed down the meal, mopping up every last drop. Good spicy smells had wafted their way up to where he was hiding out all day, in an old shack by the logging spot. Grace was serving warm apple cake for dessert. Margot was following with cream to pour over the top. Cody had his fork ready. Grace set the sumptuous dessert before him. Margot was in the middle of asking if he wanted cream when Millie came and whisked the warm, spicy goodness right out from in front of him. "We will keep you fed, dear, but dessert is for those who do their share."

.An hour or so after supper, everyone was relaxing around the hearth when Max said, "Anyone hearin' noises out back?" They all went quiet, listening. Thunk. Thunk. Thunk.

"Hmmm, I'll go check," said Silas. He wasn't surprised to see his boy out there, a lamp hanging on the post, and nearly all the rest of the woodpile neatly stacked.

No one took notice of Millie slipping off into the kitchen. When she didn't return, Silas said, "I'll go check." She had carried a tray out back, holding two plates of apple cake and two black coffees. She sat on the splitting stump and Cody on an uncut log across from her, enjoying cake, sipping coffee.

Silas stayed in the shadows on the back porch, unnoticed, and smiled at the sight. *So like Millie. Thank you, Lord, for this family—for my family.*

Millie finished her dessert, took a sip of coffee, and broke the silence. "Cody, when you lived out in California, did you ever see the ocean?"

Cody stared at her for a minute. "Yeah, I seen it. We lived by it for a while, 'fore we got to Frisco."

Millie leaned forward. "What's it like?"

"Ya mean ya never seen the ocean?"

Millie smiled. "Maybe never will, but it's kind of a dream of mine to see it. Someday."

"Well," he began, "it's really big. *Really* big. You cain't even see the end of it. Not even the edges!" He went on, energized. Nobody had ever asked him about anything before. "Mostly it looks calm and sparkly, but if it's a'stormin', that ol' ocean churns up some mighty big waves. It can be real scary. Real scary."

"Oh my goodness!" Millie exclaimed. "It's a crazy dream, but I sure would like ta see that big ocean someday." She gazed off in the distance. "What about you, Cody? What's your crazy dream?" She looked at him earnestly.

"Me? Oh, I ain't got no dreams. None that would come true."

"How do you know? It don't hurt ta dream, ya know."

For the first time in his short life, as Cody lay in his bunk that night, he dared to wonder what his dream might be.

Chapter 24

Kate had recovered, and except for a bit of backache, she was feeling wonderful. The October sun felt good as she sat on the porch, the rocking chair propped with pillows, stitching a baby gown. She figured she had a good month to get fully prepared for the new addition.

Max had taken Jake to work with him, horseback no less. He looked so tiny sitting in front of his father on Solomon. Kate was grateful when he'd brought her long-lost trunk back from the place Silas had stashed it. Her garments were musty from the dampness, but washed and sun-bleached, the cottons made fine baby clothes. And books. She'd forgotten about several volumes of poetry. She thought it would be good to introduce the boys to poetry when she got back to teaching. Grace was doing a wonderful job in the meantime. She had added French to the curriculum. Kate smiled at the thought of it. She was grateful, happy, and content.

Needing more thread, she stood to go inside. Without warning, a sharp pain nearly knocked her to her knees. "Ohhh!" she cried out, trying to take a step. It hit her again, a crashing pain. She stumbled to the corner post and hung on for dear life, scanning the place for Max. For *anybody*. "Ohhh! Dear God!" Once again the intense pain came, then a consciousness of warm fluid. *The baby. Help me, Lord. Bring someone, please!*

In the distance, she spotted Cody off from the others, teaching Goliath to fetch. "Cody," she yelled as loudly as she could. "Cody!" Desperately she called. He shaded his eyes, finally looking her way. She had gone to her knees with the last contraction. Cody trotted halfway toward her before he realized something was terribly wrong.

"Get Max! Millie too," Kate frantically shouted. "The baby—hurry, Cody, please hurry."

Cody took off like a bullet, the pup barely able to keep up. He leaped a fence and ran faster than lightning through the field, bare feet not slowing him a bit. Josh and Joey were hauling a bucket of milk out of the barn. "Where's Max?" Cody shouted, breathless.

"They're all at the church—" Cody was gone before Josh finished the sentence.

He burst into the church, face red as a beet, sucking air. "Miss Kate's having the baby!" Max and Millie didn't stop for questions, but raced madly out the door. Cody bent over with his hands on knees, thinking he would barf. At last he caught his breath and looked up.

There stood Silas, holding little Jake. "Ya done real good, son. Real good."

Millie made it just in time, shouting orders to Max while she got busy acting as a midwife. By the time he got the water boiling, raced to the inn for supplies, and returned, the child had arrived. Millie directed Max to wait a bit while she arranged mother and baby for presentation.

At last Max was allowed inside the bedroom. Kate looked radiant, even though wisps of damp hair stuck to her face, results of the work she had just done. The tiny babe in her arms was swaddled in a blue blanket. Tears sprung up in Max's eyes. "He's so tiny. Is he gonna be all right? Are you all right, Katy?" She was very tired, but couldn't stop the giggles. "Kate?"

"Come closer, Max. Meet your daughter."

That evening, Liz, Ada, and Pearl insisted on tending to Kate and the baby, while Max, Josh, Joey, and Jake went over to the inn for supper. Of course the twins were ecstatic about their "baby sister," and even more so that she was named Ruth, after their mother. Ruth Kathryn Reed would in very short order become Ruthie K.

After supper, as warm huckleberry cobbler was being served, Millie directed Grace to give Cody two servings. "You deserve extra tonight son."

"That's for sure!" exclaimed Freddie, who had witnessed the run. "Never saw anybody run like that."

Max said, "I sure do thank ya, Cody. You're a hero in my book."

Silas was beaming.

Millie pulled up a chair across from the boy. "How in the world did ya become such a fast runner?"

Cody shrugged, huckleberry juice running down his chin. "I dunno. Prolly all my years runnin' from the law." Had it not been the sad truth, it might have been funny. No one laughed.

"Repeat after me," Miss Grace instructed. "Un, deux, trois."

Of course, Andre and Louie already knew French, but they were willing to go along and even demonstrate the pronunciation of certain French sounds. "Un, deux, trois," Andre repeated with extra emphasis.

"Ooon, derr, traw," the class said in unison. Andre looked at Grace and shrugged, silently suggesting they weren't making much progress.

Grace began again. "Everyone watch my lips." Sam was already watching them. "Let's take *deux*. Altogether, say eeeeeee"

They all said, "Eeeeee."

"Good! Now say it again with your lips puckered like you're going to whistle." She demonstrated. "Eee-yooo." All five faced her intently. "Eee-yooo." They were serious, even Cody. Josh and Joey's eyebrows knit every time they said it. "Eee-yooo."

Something about the ragtag bunch made Grace smile. They kept on doing it. She looked at each face as they sat before her: Louie, Josh, Samuel, then Andre, Cody, and Joe. Grace couldn't help but chuckle at the sight. "Eeee-yooo," they said again.

"All right, class, that's—it's good for—" Abruptly she turned to face away from them, hand over mouth, shoulders shaking with laughter. She couldn't quit.

The boys went quiet and then on cue, "Eeee-yooo," sending her into another fit of giggles. Every time she took a deep breath, trying to collect herself, the boys made her laugh again.

Thankfully, Millie kicked open the kitchen door, carrying a big tray. "*Sticky* buns!" she announced with gusto.

———

The harvest moon that night was spectacular as Samuel and Grace went for a stroll after supper. Samuel looked straight ahead and asked, "You happy now?"

"Yes, much happier, Samuel, and thank you for your prayers. It means a lot."

"*Merci beaucoup* for your prayers too." His smile was bright in the moonlight.

She laughed. "You are a very good student."

"You very good teacher." They walked in silence a while, and then Samuel stopped and turned toward her. "Would you show me way to say that again? Sound we learn today?"

She smiled, hoping she wouldn't get the giggles. "Eeee-yooo," she said, looking right at him, her lips puckered, her hair silvery like a halo in the moon's shimmer. Their eyes held. Samuel didn't know the French or English word for what he felt, but he knew she felt it too. Very gently he took her shoulders, pulled her to him, brushing her lips with his own. He embraced her more fully. She didn't resist, but wrapped her arms around him too.

"You very beautiful teacher," he whispered and kissed her again, this time deeply, lingering.

That night Grace snuggled beneath her downy quilts, her body tired but her mind wide awake. She could think only about Samuel, the kiss they shared, the warmth she felt just thinking about it—about him. She loved the way he looked at her and the way he was always positive, always in a happy mood. He was grateful for the smallest thing. She loved that about him. She loved everything about him. *I think I'm in love with him.*

———

When Ada took a turn holding sweet Ruthie, Will showed up on Kate's front porch, waiting for her to join him. There weren't enough porches to go around, it appeared. Freddie emerged right behind Will to ask after Liz. By the time Max got back home, only Pearl was with Kate, and the two sisters seemed to be having a delightful time fixing lace and ribbon around the baby girl's downy head.

Meanwhile, back at the inn, Millie and Silas had taken over that porch, as was their custom each night after supper. It was a moment they both cherished, the time when they could share their long day, their hopes and dreams. Millie had come to rely on Silas: his strength, the sweet way he treated her. And Silas had never loved anyone the way he loved Millie.

They were sitting there with mugs of coffee, marveling at the harvest moon, when creaking sounds from behind announced a visitor. It was Cody, slipping out the front door. "Well, look who's here!" Millie exclaimed. "Pull up a chair, darlin'." Silas looked none too happy when the boy wrangled another rocker right between them.

"What you guys talkin' about?"

Silas thought, *Oh great. Right when I was gettin' up ma nerve ta talk serious to Millie.*

"We were just sayin' that's the biggest harvest moon we'd either one ever seen," said Millie.

"Yep, it shor is a humdinger," Cody replied.

"What about you, Cody?" Millie asked. "Ya figure out that crazy dream yet?"

"Not exactly, but got a few idears. For now, though, I'm needin' to buy me a horse. Wonderin' if ya could maybe give me extra work? It don't need ta be a fancy horse, just sound and not too old."

Millie was perplexed. "Got any thoughts on the matter, Silas?"

Silas rubbed his scruffy chin. "Well now, ya mind sayin' why ya need a horse, son?"

"Well," Cody hesitated then leaned toward Silas, whispering. "Could I have a word with ya, around the corner?"

Silas cleared his throat. "Millie, honey, me and Cody's gonna fetch some hot coffee. Hand me your cup, sweetheart. We'll be right back."

A few minutes later, Silas returned saying the boy had gone on to the bunkhouse. Millie asked, "Well, why in the world does he need a horse, for goodness' sake?"

Silas chuckled. "I reckon it's all right ta say. He didn't exactly swear me to secrecy, and besides, he figures it'll be nearly three years."

"Three years till what?" Millie was utterly confounded.

"Three years till he can manage the trip."

"Silas, tell me! Trip to where? What's this about?" She looked troubled.

"He says he's takin' you out ta Californey. Wants ya ta see the ocean."

Chapter 25

Ruthie K turned five months old the following March and was the spitting image of her mama. Everyone fussed over the pretty little thing. She would be dedicated to the Lord on the coming Sunday, the first official occurrence in the new building. The windows had been hung, and the men, at last, were putting up the cross. All the boys, including Cody and Samuel, had put their heart and soul into the construction of it, leaving it to weather in the elements. Max had fabricated some brackets at the shop to hang it. Millie and Kate—all the women, in fact—were instructed not to look until it was time.

"What on earth is takin' so long?" Millie asked nobody in particular. Fresh-baked cookies were piled on trays, covered with linens, awaiting the celebration of the completion of God's House. That's what they would call it. That day they would gather at the church to dedicate the building to the Lord. There were no pews or benches, and no preacher yet, but Millie and Silas planned out where Silas would say a few words, two or three would pray, and the congregation would sing a hymn.

Everyone washed up. The menfolk put on clean shirts, and the ladies, their Sunday dresses, in honor of the Lord.

At last it was time. Millie and Silas led the unlikely band of brothers and sisters, a colorful divergence of folks, young and old, dark and light, reminding Grace of God's beautiful blanket. They were bubbling with excitement, jabbering, laughing all the way. But as each one entered God's House, a hush fell over them. They gathered midway into the empty place, speechless at what they saw. The low afternoon sun slanting through tall windows cast a brilliant glow on the wall behind the pulpit. Against that golden background stood the cross. It seemed to tower above the crowd, its rustic beauty captivating. The Spirit of God settled over that small assembly. Silas took Millie's hand. Max took Kate's.

Grace was overwhelmed with a sense of love, surrounded by that family, in that building—God's House. Tears flowed freely as she gazed on the cross. *The cross. You never left me, Lord. In all my scattered life, You were there. I was in a hopeless place, near death, but You surrounded me with Your angels.* She closed her eyes and with a shaky voice quietly began to sing. "I once was lost—but now I'm found—was blind but now I see." Samuel took her hand. Her sweet voice grew stronger, echoing as it reverberated off the high ceiling.

Simone's and Margot's melodious voices joined in, and then Kate's and Millie's. The men's deep voices added richness and filled the building. "'Twas grace that taught my heart to fear and grace my fears relieved; how precious did that grace appear the hour I first believed."

Silas remembered Kate singing that hymn the day God got ahold of him. Millie was overwhelmed with gratitude that her beautiful Grace had come home. She had prayed for nearly twenty years. *Praise you, Lord.* Max, glancing over at Kate, still couldn't believe God had brought her to him, literally out of the blue, and had blessed them with beautiful children.

Glimpsing over his shoulder, Max observed Josh and Joey standing off to the side, singing earnestly, looking suddenly taller. He was so proud of his young brothers. Cody was next to them, listening, eyes fixed on the cross. Samuel, with tears streaming, still smiled his big smile, remembering how two matching boys brought him to a new family—a new life. And now sweet Grace. *Thank you, Jesus.*

Simone recalled the way the Lord had protected her and Pale Moon, running for their lives, nearly starving to death. It was amazing the way Pierre had stumbled onto them in the middle of nowhere. And Silas had shown up on their front steps. *You truly work in mysterious ways, Lord.*

Having forgotten about their planned program, quietly they walked back to the inn. Millie suggested that since the day was still warm, they enjoy cookies and tea on the porch. The men brought out a table, and soon it was spread with a cloth and trays of cookies, along with pitchers of sweet tea. Slowly the conversation picked up, the women sitting in rockers, the men and boys milling around the cookie table or sitting on the steps.

Silas brought tea to Millie and sat down next to her on a bench near the end of the porch. "Think we should tell 'em? Is now a good time?"

Millie replied anxiously, "Well, I guess now is good as any."

Just as Silas stood and cleared his throat to speak, Samuel, at the other end of the porch, spoke first. "Everybody? I like to say announcement please." Max motioned him to stand in front of everyone, facing the porch. Grace followed, and he took her hand. Samuel looked at her and took a deep breath. "Miss Grace has accepted me for uh—" He looked at her again and smiled, his dark eyes dancing. "We get married soon."

There was silence, then everyone erupted in cheers and congratulations for the happy couple. Millie smiled up at Silas, who look dumbfounded. "Well, bless Pat."

She squeezed his hand. "Silas, darlin', let's wait for our news. Let Gracie and Samuel have their day. Look how happy they are." The irony of it settled on Millie. Indians had long ago taken her Gracie, and now she would soon be giving Grace away to an Indian. But Samuel was truly a good man. He was truly a Christian. She could see how well he loved Grace.

Max finally got the chance to sit by Kate, little Ruthie sleeping in her arms. He smiled at the lovely sight, his girls. He sighed and said, "What a day this has been!" The late-afternoon sun brought a rosy glow to the scene before them. Pierre and Simone and Margot laughing joyfully, the three Montague boys, Josh, Joey, and Cody, Freddie and Liz, Ada and Will, and Pearl, all surrounding Samuel and Grace. Millie and Silas finally got a turn to give their blessing.

Max said, "We have a mighty wonderful family out there, Katy."

"Yes, we do Max. It's just a little taste of heaven."

All of a sudden, a commotion from behind the building erupted. Little Jake was running for all his worth toward the crowd. All five pups were after him. "No, no doddy! Top it, Petie. Bad doddy." Since he couldn't tell them apart, he called them all Petie. In the melee, his britches slipped, and Petie got a hold of his pant leg. "No! Petie!" Jake was now squealing at the top of his lungs and headed for the only mud puddle for miles around, just behind the crowd.

"Better get him, Max," Kate said with urgency, feeling helpless with the baby and all. Max parted the crowd, which by then was captivated by the unfolding drama. Before Max got there, Jake hit the puddle, along with all five dogs yipping, their owners calling them frantically. Petie, Andy, James, and AJ paid no attention, but to everyone's amazement, Goliath sat on his haunches then turned woefully and went to Cody.

Jake, having slipped, now sat in the mud, screaming. The pups were jumping all over him with muddy paws. When Max hit the edge of the big puddle, one of the pups attacked his pant leg, causing him to go off balance and slip. He fell on his rump in the puddle, next to Jake. He landed sitting up, but by then he was laughing so hard he just lay down and let the pups have at it. Jake climbed up on his father's belly, adding more mud. He seemed to forget about the pups. "Diddy up, ho-see."

Kate handed poor Ruthie over to Liz on her way to rescue Jake—and Max. She picked up Jake and held him at arm's length, all the way around back to the pump. Josh and Joey ran to Max's aid. They knew they were in trouble for not minding their dogs, and they each grabbed an arm, hoping to get in his good graces. Before they knew it, Max had pulled each of them into the mud instead. He knew Kate would be irate at the laundry he was causing, but it was worth it.

The crowd was laughing hysterically as Kate rounded the corner, packing a scrubbed Jake wrapped in a clean tablecloth. "What's going on?" she asked. She slipped between Silas and Cody, then gasped at the sight. There sat Max, Josh, Joe, and the four puppies in the middle of the puddle, covered head to toe with mud, laughing like lunatics.

"Max!" she shouted. "What on earth?"

He could barely quit laughing long enough to answer. "You said it, sweetheart. You said it. Just a little taste of heaven."

Chapter 26

The day was perfect: crisp but clear and sunny, sky as blue as Millie's eyes. "Oh, Silas, this day will go down as one of my happiest." They had gone over early to get the fire started to make sure the church building was warm and ready. The boys were on a mission to pick buckets of wildflowers, the choicest to be tied for the bride's bouquet. The circuit preacher had come in the day before. The wedding would take place at noon, followed by a sumptuous buffet dinner.

Samuel looked handsome, his warm brown skin against a crisp white shirt and Max's dark-blue coat. His black hair was tied back with a leather strip. His eyes were like rich coffee. And there was that ever-present smile.

The crowd was stunned when Grace walked in, Pierre on one arm and Silas on the other. She wore full Indian dress: soft doeskin bleached nearly white with long fringe—at least a foot—at the hem and sleeves. The dress was heavily beaded with various shades of blue, red, and coral in a design that ran the full length of it.

Simone had created it over time, waiting for that day. Margot had fashioned her moccasins of the same white doeskin, beaded as the dress and matching headband. Grace's dazzling silvery-golden hair hung thick and straight nearly to her waist. Her blue eyes glistened with unshed tears as she looked up at Samuel. In that moment, his face sobered. In the same moment, Grace broke into a smile that took his breath away.

After the wedding, they moved into Reed's cabin out back, Millie insisting the furniture from Grace's bedroom be theirs, a wedding gift of sorts. But the real gift was that Millie had hired a photographer from Cheyenne to take their wedding picture. Before the gent left, he had captured not only a lovely portrait of the bride and groom, but also Millie, Silas, and Cody, the Montague family, the Reed family, and the whole lot of them in one big photograph framed and hanging over the inn's fireplace.

Millie was gazing at that family portrait when Kate slipped in early one morning. A cozy fire was just beginning to crackle, and lamps on the mantle had been lit. Kate waited quietly in the background, knowing Millie was deep in prayer—a prayer of thanksgiving, she was sure. When Millie turned and saw her, she hurried over and pulled Kate into her arms. "Oh, Katy, I was just thanking the Lord for you."

"For me?" Kate was astonished. "Me?"

"God knows how grateful I am to have my precious Grace again and the blessing of her marriage to such a fine man as Samuel. But you coming into my life when you did—you were my lifesaver. You were the glue that kept me together as hope had faded. I felt like you were a daughter to me, not to replace Grace, of course, but one to help fill the emptiness inside me."

Kate was speechless. She looked into Millie's blue eyes, now brimming with tears. "Dear Millie, you're the one. You've been like the mother I've missed for so long, like a nurse graciously caring for me. For Papa. All I am today; I owe to you. I love you, Millie Thatcher."

"And I love you, sweet girl." They both broke down, crying, laughing, sniffling, and hugging. Then Millie smiled brightly. "Let's go for a walk."

Cody hadn't meant to listen. He had come in the back to check on firewood and had stopped in the kitchen for a cup of coffee.

This is the craziest place I've ever seen. These people really care about each other. They love each other. All of 'em. He stepped through the kitchen door after Millie and Kate went out the front, and walked over to the hearth.

For a very long time, Cody stood staring at the portrait, looking at each face. Mindlessly he sipped his coffee, recalling the way each of those people had shown him much kindness. How curious that the photographer had placed him directly in the middle, surrounded by that big family. *Me. A filthy little homeless hooligan, a robber and a thief.* Cody had some kind of feeling come over him. He couldn't quite figure it out. Something warm, peaceful. He glanced down to see one of the cats lying curled up by the warmth of the fire, purring. He chuckled. "That's just how I feel, kitty. Like purring."

———

The June morning air was cool and fresh. Kate and Millie were walking back toward the inn, arm and arm, laughing like schoolgirls. In the other direction, Cody saw Josh and Joey splitting wood and little Jake stacking the split logs slowly, one at a time. Ruthie was trying to catch a chicken, while Max, with Annie on his back, doctored a horse. Out beyond the back pasture he could see the Montague boys helping Sam build a shed and Grace, Simone, and Margot drinking coffee on the porch, laughing happily. Their stitching baskets were close at hand.

As Cody walked toward the pen, where a strong-willed colt awaited his attention, Silas came out of the barn. "Cody! Hey, son. I been lookin' for ya." Silas walked alongside Cody, his hand clapped on the boy's shoulder. "Tomorrow, what d'ya say we take the day off and go huntin'? I got a gut feelin' George is hangin' around these parts."

"George?" All kinds of thoughts crossed Cody's mind, the main one being that George was some kind of outlaw.

"King George. The biggest bull elk you ever laid eyes on."

"Really? Oh man. That'd be great!"

Cody walked to the pen, whistling. He felt happy. He was part of a family—a family that loved him. He didn't know for sure if he was talking to God or to himself, but with all his heart he made a promise right then and there. *One of these days, some way, somehow, I'm gonna do somethin' for these people—my family. Somethin' big!*

When Millie stepped out back to clang the dinner bell, she couldn't help but smile. The signs of a hard day's work were evident in every direction. Wood was piled high, horses were trimmed and shod, butter was churned, bedding was washed and hanging on the line. And over in the pen, there sat Cody in a saddle on the back of Buckshot, the most cantankerous colt on earth. He waved at Millie, a big smile on his sweat-streaked face. Millie wanted to hug him with everything she had. But she swallowed the lump in her throat and waved back. "I knew you'd do it, Cody!"

She thought, *Can't quite recall if it was Kate or Max that said it first, Lord, but it's true. This life, in this place, at this time is just a little taste of heaven. For that, I'm so very thankful, Lord.*

"Time ta eat, son!"

Part Three

LILA PENROSE

*"He brought me up out of an horrible pit, out of the miry clay,
and set my feet upon a rock, and established my goings."*
Psalm 40:2

Chapter 27

San Francisco, 1868

Lila Penrose always milked the cow and gathered eggs early on Sundays. Her father insisted the family get to church one hour before the congregation, start the fire, sweep the porch, and pray.

It was a typical cool San Francisco morning, with fog settled on the bay. She spotted something and stopped in her tracks. Something or some*body* was behind the chicken coop. Then she saw boots. Men's boots, somebody lying there. She walked backward toward the house, never taking her eyes off the boots.

"Did ya bring the eggs, Lila?" her mother called.

Lila backed into the screen door. "There's a man out there," she said in hushed tones.

"What d'ya say, girl?"

Lila ran inside, slamming the back door shut. She leaned against it like her petite fourteen-year-old form could keep it that way. "Papa!" the girl shouted. Esther Penrose looked out the window and reached for the shotgun over the door at the same time.

"What's the fuss?" Pastor Ike grumbled as he came in the kitchen, tucking in his Sunday shirt.

"There's a man sleeping behind the chicken house, not moving."

The pastor took the gun and walked cautiously out toward the chicken coop while mother and daughter nervously watched, hand in hand.

"He's still breathin'," he conveyed. "But we best get him inside." With the help of Brother Jackson, who happened to be heading up to church, they got the stranger laid out on a cot in the back room. "Don't reckon he's long for this world," the preacher said. "I best stay with him. Davey Smith can lead the folks in hymns this morning."

Throughout the morning, the stranger stirred, blinked his eyes a few times as if trying to speak, but passed out each time, his breathing labored. He was in bad shape and in dire need of a bath. Ike Penrose, pastor of the Hillside Methodist Church, rather than waste a good sermon went ahead and began preaching as he sat by the bedside, shotgun close at hand.

About midway through, the slumbering stranger said with a ragged voice, "Map." Then he drifted off again. A bit later, he tried to move, and his face contorted with pain. "Map—under—stone." A wracking cough left him limp, wheezing. "Give—my—son." That would be his last words.

———

Silas pounded the final spike, gave a whoop, and the crowd cheered. Over the past two years, much had happened. The General Store was up and running and of course the church, God's House, was in full swing. The men had recently put up a long-awaited wooden sign: "Welcome to Thatcher Springs." Millie was ecstatic. Her vision of a real town was coming to fruition.

Government land had become available for homesteading, and Max paid the fee to claim 160 acres to the east end across the road from the inn. With everyone pitching in, he built a log house that would better accommodate his growing family, which included Josh and Joe, now tall and lanky, Jake, Ruthie K, and little Annie Grace.

The Montague family claimed a parcel about a mile to the west and built a log home as well, similar to the one they left behind. Pierre had discovered untouched trapping country between their new home and the Fur Trading Company he sold to, up north.

Silas and Millie tied the knot six months after Sam and Grace's ceremony, which was the first wedding in God's House. "Silas, honey, did you ever in your life see a more beautiful bride than our Grace?" Millie had been asking this ever since the wedding, to which Silas always replied, "Only the one I'm lookin' at now, darlin'."

A few months later, Will and Ada had a simple ceremony and headed back east, where his family planned a grand reception. They had been wanting to discuss the idea of Will becoming a partner in the steamship business. Eventually, Freddie and Liz married and went back to Kansas to take over the Alexander ranch, the tenant unable to continue for poor health.

Millie was a quarter of the way into her ninety-nine-year, US government lease of the inn. It had been officer's quarters of an intended army fort, but was abandoned before completion. With the establishment of Indian reservations, there was no longer a need for army reinforcements in Idaho Territory. It was just Millie, Henry, and a couple of drifters she'd hired in exchange for room and board that got the place up and running—but mostly Millie. The building was solid and included a mixed lot of furniture.Millie turned it into a reputable inn—no ordinary stagecoach stop. With the sign being hung, she was inspired to give the old place a facelift. Before bad weather, she would arrange a little white-washing party.

———

Midweek, Pastor Ike called a meeting of the men of Hillside Methodist. "Before undertaker Billy Jack hauled off the body, we searched his clothes and boots for some way to identify him, but there weren't none. Kept nothin' but his belt, a good piece of leather."

Brother Jesse spoke up. "I'm a thinkin' only thang ta figure is them words he spoke. All's we got to go on."

"Yep, I reckon if we could figure out where's the map", Brother Clyde said, "and the stone". He scratched his head. What in tarnation is that sposed ta mean? There's a billion stones right on this here hill!"

Pastor Ike scratched his own head and sighed. "I dunno what ta do, but I feel an obligation to the poor soul—and his son, whoever he is. My Lila Jane suggested we each one pick a word he spoke and pray over it. Maybe God will show us."

"Well, least it's a idear,'" Jesse said. "I'll pick *son*."

"Well, fer heaven sake, Jesse, pick *my son*. Nobody's gonna want ta pray for *my* with nothin' else hooked to it."

After quite a bit of squabbling, the men went home with a word to pray over, having agreed to meet again after church on Sunday. They decided to have the women bring some dishes and make a potluck out of it.

———

Cody had a way with animals. This was apparent with his dog, Goliath; the runt was now the biggest of the bunch. But it wasn't just the dog. Cody had a natural ability with horses, along with all he'd learned from Max, who had gained so much from Henry. Cody spent long hours training, patiently coaxing the best out of some of Max's worst.

Max had given him his choice of horses from a string of seven, for his own, in exchange for work. The big black, Warrior, was his pick. He was tall, strong, and fast. Cody loved to run him on the wagon trail, keeping track of his time with Clayton Alexander's pocket watch. Warrior kept getting faster and faster. The crazy old boy loved to run.

One sunny June morning, Cody happened on Max talking with the Pony Express rider, his horse in tow. *That's strange*, he said to himself. *Pony Express don't even slow down.* As Cody approached the two men, the reason was obvious. The Express horse was lame, evidently having stepped in a rut. Max was in the middle of saying, "Well, not unless you can cut a deal with Cody here."

Cody stepped up to where the men were talking. "What about me?"

"Roy's lookin' to buy a fresh pony that can run. Told him maybe you'd be interested, seein's how Warrior's the fastest horse on the place, bar none."

Roy said, "I got a deadline ta meet. I'll give ya cash, two hundred dollars right now."

Max slanted a look at Cody, thinking, *He's put his heart and soul into that horse; he'll never let him go.*

Cody was deliberating .

Roy said, "What d'ya say kid? I gotta git."

Nobody said a thing for a moment, then Cody said, "Four hundred."

After Roy looked the horse over, they settled on two hundred dollars then, and two hundred delivered next trip, if the horse was fast as claimed. A quick receipt was written up and a quick IOU, subject to the horse's performance. After Roy transferred his mailbags, he gave Warrior a kick in the ribs and took off like a bolt of lightning. *Yes sir, that old boy sure does love ta run,* Cody thought.

Chapter 28

Months had passed since Pastor Ike and the men of Hillside Methodist started praying over the last words of that stranger behind Penrose's chicken coop. They'd had a couple of leads, but those had fizzled.

It seemed extra quiet on the early morning of October 21. Esther was just setting out breakfast when she felt the first tremor. The dishes in the china cupboard tinkled then began rattling off the shelves. Gramma Penrose's teapot fell to the floor and shattered.

"Ike? *Lila!*" she screamed.

They scrambled in from chores. "Under the table," Ike ordered. "Quick!" The big oak table was the sturdiest thing in the house. It had protected them before. They huddled there, Lila tucked between her parents. Breakfast now lay on the floor among the broken plates.

When the earth finally stopped shaking, each was praying, not only for their own safety, but also for the congregation, whom they loved like family, and for the church building. *Lord, may it still be standin',* Lila prayed.. *And, Lord, I pray my violin survived.*

The violin did survive. It had flown off its perch and landed on her featherbed. As mother and daughter were sweeping up the mess in the house, Ike had gone to check on the church.

"The church is still standin', praise God! Even the bell tower made it this time. Kind of a mess inside though, a broke window,

150

stuff scattered about. If ya haven't looked out front yet, our porch fell off. Again. The barn's good. Chicken coop's a gonner; chickens ever'where. The cemetery took a hit though. Markers scattered about, tombstones down. Some broke in half. Us men of the congregation got our work cut out, for sure."

Esther couldn't help but check the back porch. *Praise the Lord! It's still in one piece.* It was the most significant spot on the place, as far as Esther was concerned. It was screened-in to keep the pests out, and there she could sit for a spell and read her Bible or do some stitching. Those were times of refreshing.

But that wasn't the main reason she loved the back porch. Since many of their parishioners couldn't tithe money, they left gifts there: a bushel of apples or jugs of cider from Andersons' orchard; potatoes, onions, corn, and carrots from Millers' garden and baked goods from Ursula Stephen's bakery. The town seamstress, Susanna Larson, would leave remnants of fabric, a wonderful blessing to Esther, a fine seamstress herself.

But those weren't the main reasons Esther loved the back porch. She would never forget that Sunday, so long ago. They had been to church and afterward, as customary, Ike had sat to rest on the front porch, while Esther went inside to fetch some sweet tea. She was heading back out when a little nudge made her stop, set the tea down, and check the back porch. It was often on Sunday something special showed up. She stepped out the back door, hoping Ursula had left a small cake or sugar cookies to serve with the tea. There sat a basket she hadn't seen before. Puzzled, she bent over it and lifted the white linen.

"Oh dear God!" she said aloud and dropped to her knees. It was a baby. Esther began to cry. And laugh. She just sat on her knees, rocking back and forth, afraid to pick it up. *A baby!* How she had prayed for a child. How she had tried to accept that she and Ike would never have children. The tiny babe blinked her eyes open and looked up at Esther, so helpless, so dependent.

Esther marshaled her courage and gathered up the sweet infant. "Who are you, little one?" She held the babe close, gently patting her back. Through her tears, she could barely read a note attached to the basket. *I know you will love her and teach her the things of God.* That was all.

Esther was crying tears of joy, still on her knees, rocking the babe, when Ike found her. A fresh flood of tears engulfed her as she looked up at him. "Oh, Ike. Ike! God brought us a daughter!"

Lila Jane was beautiful in every way, inside and out. She tied her curly red hair back most of the time, to keep it from springing wildly. Except for a scatter of freckles, her skin was like peaches and cream, complementing the golden hazel of her eyes. She was quiet, studious, loved God's Word and poetry, and played the violin like an angel. Since the church had no piano or organ, on Sunday mornings Lila played hymns—hauntingly beautiful hymns—on her violin. Yes, God had truly blessed Esther and Ike.

———

The family was sleeping soundly in the wee hours of the morning when all at once Ike sat straight up in bed. "That's *it*! Glory be. That's gotta be it."

"What on earth are you talkin' about, Ivan?" Esther called him Ivan when upset with him.

Lila stumbled in from her room. "What is it, Papa?"

"The *stone*! He must've meant a *head*stone, out in the cemetery. Why didn't we think of it before?" Ike jumped up and started pulling on his britches.

"You can't go out there now, for heaven's sake. Wait at least till daylight." Esther was always the more sensible one.

"I just can't believe it. Why none of us ever thought of *head*stone. And bein' we found him back of the chicken coop makes sense he was comin' from the graveyard. And the really strange thing, *stone* ain't even my word. It's Clyde's."

———

Cody had money, and lots of it. Roy, the Pony Express rider, had made good on his IOU, making it a total of four hundred bucks for Warrior. It was Cody's ticket out of there. He didn't need to stay in what he considered a desolate place in the middle of nowhere, with a bunch of Bible thumpers. He could go west, back to California or maybe Oregon—or Kansas City, or even the East Coast. He had enough greenbacks to leave Thatcher Springs.

But he *had* promised Millie that she would see the ocean. It was her dream, after all. Cody still didn't know what his own dream was, but he figured he'd go ahead with the promise. He had to admit, she had been awful good to him—better than his own mother. He'd hide the cash under the mattress. Only Max knew about his money from the sale of Warrior, and that's how Cody wanted to keep it.

It was a warm evening, but pleasant for porch sitting. It seemed to Millie that Cody had joined them more often than not lately. Just the three of them: Silas, Millie, and Cody.

Right when he was going to bring up traveling west, Millie broke into his thinking. "Cody dear, me and Silas have somethin' to discuss with ya."

Uh oh. I must be in trouble.

Silas said, "You been doin' real good, son. Workin' hard, doin' yer studies, fittin' in real good. Ya even quit cussin', far as I can tell. Millie here is gettin' real attached to ya. And me? I'm shore proud ta be your adopted pa."

Oh no, here it comes. They're gonna tell me ta git baptized.

"We want to make the adoption permanent, legal. We want you to be our true legal son."

Millie took hold of his hand when she said, "Me and Silas, we love ya, son."

Cody was speechless, stupefied. "Uh, well then, would I have a different name?"

"Well," Millie began, "only if ya want."

Silas added, "We was thinkin' maybe Cody Walton Mitchell."

They couldn't read the boy. He just sat there, looking down.

"Why don't ya sleep on it, sweetie," Millie suggested. "And pray about it," she added.

Cody spoke with Max the next morning. "Did you tell anybody about the money? Like Silas and Millie?"

"I haven't told a soul. It's your business, Cody, and I respect that," Max replied. "But I do have ta say, you drive a hard bargain." Max smiled. "And I respect that too."

Cody almost asked him for advice on the adoption but decided he needed to figure it out for himself. "Sleepin' on it" wasn't working though, because Cody hadn't slept all night. He was mixed up. Should he just take off? Where would he go? If he stayed, what would he do? What was his dream? Maybe being a famous horse trainer? Or starting his own cow herd like Max had done? But he knew that wouldn't work. He wasn't old enough to stake a claim, unless he got married—and he knew that'd be a cold day. They said they loved him. He wondered why. Nobody had ever told him that before. He thought, *Couldn't be right, but couldn't be about the money either, if Max didn't tell 'em.* Cody knew he needed somebody to talk to.

Millie said to pray about it, Cody thought. "If I did, you wouldn't probably listen," he said to the ceiling. "Just wish I had a clear sign what ta do. Um, God, if yer up there—"

Chapter 29

About midday, Cody spotted a cloud of dust in the distance, which turned out to be Warrior going full out with Roy on his back.

"Love this ol' pony, Cody!" Roy shouted as he tossed a package and took off in a whirlwind.

Cody untied the string to find three letters, one addressed to him. *What in the world?* Hurriedly he set out for the bunkhouse, which he knew would be empty that time of day. He put the other mail on the kitchen table, where Millie would see it. Once alone, he plopped on the bunk and ripped open the letter. It was neatly addressed to the son of Franklin S. Walton.

March 11, 1873

Dear Mr. Walton,

This letter is to inform you that your father, Franklin S. Walton, passed away in the year 1868. His Last Will and Testament is in safekeeping with Fr. Francesca Viejo, who still resides in the ruins of Mission San Jose. I have been entrusted in a rather peculiar way to convey to you a map of foremost importance. It would be in your best interest to make travel arrangements to

> *San Francisco as soon as possible. It has taken nearly*
> *five years and much prayer to find you. We look*
> *forward to your arrival.*
>
> *Sincerely yours,*
> *Lila Penrose for:*
> *Pastor Ivan Penrose*
> *Hillside Methodist Church*
> *San Francisco, California*

Cody couldn't help but wonder if the letter was an answer to his prayer that God would send him a clear sign. He decided to talk with Max about the whole thing after all.

They were sitting on a fence rail after gathering Max's cows. In a somewhat muddled way, Cody shared everything: the conversation with Silas and Millie, his thoughts of leaving, his promise to Millie, the strange letter, and even that he had "sort of prayed about it—to God."

Max let out a low whistle. "You been carryin' a heavy load there, Cody. Thank ya for sharin' it with me. Seems like God is givin' you some direction all right, the letter and all. Maybe sort it out; take first things first. Sounds like ya need ta get back to San Francisco, according to the letter. So that'd be first. And ya promised Millie to show her the ocean, so take her along. Third, if ya invited Silas too, traveling with them, spending time together, might help ya decide if ya wanta be their son. And fourth, you got the money ta do it."

Cody couldn't believe how simple Max made it sound. "Thanks, Max. I'm gonna find Millie right now and ask her." Cody jumped down, relieved, and feeling invigorated as he ran through the pasture toward the inn.

It was Lila who spotted it. She and Esther helped the men comb through debris for nearly a week. It might not have taken so long, except that Clyde and Jesse were so intrigued, they read every headstone readable.

"Well, I'll be!" exclaimed Jesse. "Listen ta this'n. *Here Lies Willy Jackson— Kilt in Shootout—July 9, 1849.*"

"That's nothin'," replied Clyde, "specially durin' them Forty-Niner days."

Jesse was bent above the next grave; the headstone had toppled over. "Well, 'ceptin' this here fella, Calvin - uh - somethin'or other was kilt in a shootout the very same day. Ha! Them boys musta kilt each other."

This went on for three days till Brother Anderson put his foot down. "Fer cryin' out loud. We got us a job ta do. Them graves been here fer years and will be another hundert. Now let's find that map."

Shortly after that, Lila called her father over to a pile of rock, evidently one of the larger tombstones, collapsed by the earthquake. "Look right in here, Papa, between these two. See in there? Among the shattered pieces? Looks like a strip of leather."

Ike got on his knees and squinted into the crevasse made by the broken marker. "Over here, boys," he shouted. "Yep, that's a piece a leather all right." Working together, they hefted the two big pieces aside and began poking in the rubble, keeping their eyes on the leather string. The men spent a good while digging out one chunk at a time, so as not to destroy the thing they were after. With backs aching and fingers numb, at long last they retrieved a leather pouch.

Esther spoke up sweetly. "Shouldn't we pray?"

The men removed their hats, and Ike prayed over the leather pouch, that the map would be in it and that they'd find the rightful owner. With caution, Ike pulled out the contents. "Praise God. We got it!"

———

As stagecoach transportation gradually gave way to the railroad, Thatcher Springs began to transform from a stage stop to a real town. Not a depot, but an easy drive by buggy from the proposed train station midway from Ft. Laramie. The Montague family was in the process of building their own retail establishment, which would offer custom fur coats, rugs and blankets, and leather goods, including chinks, chaps, clothing, and moccasins. A saddle maker traveling through was considering collaborating with them.

The inn became Thatcher Springs Hotel and Dinner House, just a fancy name for the same place, and Millie had convinced Tom Carter to return as head cook. He brought along his younger brother, Gus.

Even though Grace and Sam were expecting their first child soon, they were making plans to build a schoolhouse. Grace reasoned she could easily teach with a papoose on her back.

The whole town couldn't wait for the new babe to arrive. With Grace being so pale and Sam so dark, everyone was contemplating what the child would look like. Millie was beside herself. *God is so good. The way he's blessed me bringin' my Grace back and givin' me a good man. And a son! Course, Cody hasn't said yes quite yet, but I truly believe it's your will, Lord. And now, a grandbaby. As Max would say, "Will wonders never cease." Thank ya, Lord Jesus. Thank ya.*

Pierre readied the wagon for their trip to the nearest Central Pacific Railroad stop, about forty miles from Thatcher Springs. Cody had purchased tickets by way of Roy of the Pony Express. He did it before even talking to Silas and Millie about it. When he did, Millie said, "Oh my, Cody. It's awful short notice. I mean, there's still guests here to deal with, and I would need ta pack and all."

Seeing a little disappointment on Cody's face, Silas stepped in. "But, Millie, sweetheart, you know how bad ya wanta see that ocean. Don't cha?"

Max, Kate, Grace, and Sam were listening from behind the kitchen door. The four walked in. "Millie, how long since ya took a trip? To anywhere?" Max asked her.

"You know, Millie," Kate added, "Grace and I can handle the inn and General Store, especially with Tom here to do the cookin'."

Grace said, "After all, Mother, you taught us well." Millie smiled inside at the word *mother*.

Sam said, "When you come back, you tell me and twinners about beeg ocean." She smiled again at the way he had picked up on calling the boys twinners.

She looked up at Silas. He said, "It'll be our first family trip!" and winked with his one good eye.

"Well," she began, "I guess we're going to California then." She added with elation, "I'm gonna see the ocean!"

Chapter 30

The thrill of the train ride and watching the scenery fly by soon gave way to the discomfort of it. The seats were hard; it was too hot during the day and too cold at night to sleep. But the three of them shared some good chats, making the time go by. Cody told them about the four hundred dollars from selling his horse and about the letter from Pastor Ike. It made Millie feel better that there was more than seeing the ocean, but she was sorry about the death of his birth father. It made adoption even more decisive though; and there would be no one to contest it. It was also unlikely his mother would ever show up.

Even though the train was three hours late pulling in to San Francisco, Pastor Ike was there waiting with horse and buggy. They agreed a good night's rest was in order before discussing the map and getting down to business.

"Just call me Ike," the preacher insisted. "It's short for Ivan. Well, actually my name's John Ivan—my ma not knowin' that Ivan is Russian for John. So technically, my name is John John. He chuckled and continued, "But everyone calls me Ike."

He delivered them to the Grand Hotel, one of San Francisco's best, where they could get a good meal, a good bed, and a good bath. When she entered the hotel, Millie completely forgot about the ocean, let alone her worries over what she'd left behind. She stood, mouth open, looking at the opulent furnishing: the rich burgundy velveteen draperies, the Oriental rugs, ornate settees, and crystal chandeliers—and that was just the lobby. She looked at Cody. "Tell me you didn't pay for stayin' here. This place must cost a fortune."

Cody grinned. "Well, jes' fer one night, Miss Millie. But don't worry none; I can afford it." He was happy he could do this for Millie and Silas. Happy even for himself. The last time he'd been in that neighborhood, it was to steal garbage. If he timed it right, he would sometimes find some extra good food scraps.

The next day, rested and refreshed, Ike picked the family up for a meeting with the men who had helped find the map. Esther and Lila would have a noon meal prepared, buffet style. Ursula had provided yeast rolls to go along with Esther's fried chicken, mashed potatoes, gravy, and glazed carrots. Lila had made the apple pies. After a most interesting trip through town, winding up a hill just outside, they came into view of the Hillside Methodist Church, the parsonage close by.

"Well, it ain't the Grand Hotel, but it's home sweet home ta me," Ike chortled.

"It's just lovely." Millie clapped her hands. She was enthralled with everything, and other than a glimpse of the foggy bay, she hadn't even seen the ocean yet. Cody was ready to get down to the business of the map: how they had found it, what his father might have said to Pastor Ike, and where the map led to. He had been wrestling over the whole thing and was about to find out the answers to many questions.

Clyde and Jess pulled up about the same time. Ike made introductions, and led the bunch through the front door. They were met with a heap of wonderful aromas coming from the kitchen.

"We're here, Esther," Ike called. Esther bustled through the kitchen door, cheeks rosy from working over a hot stove, wiping her hands on her apron.

"Do come in." She smiled brightly. "Welcome to you all." Ike introduced Silas, Millie, and Cody, and the men shook hands. Millie and Esther hugged with a kind of understanding.

"Where's Lila?" Ike asked his wife.

"She was just taking the pies from the oven to the back porch." Esther stuck her head in the kitchen. "Our guests are here, Lila."

Cody recalled that Lila had written the letter. He was thinking back on what that letter had said, when in she walked. Red curls had escaped the ribbon that held them back, framing her beautiful face. Like her mother, her cheeks were flushed, making her big hazel eyes sparkle brightly. Her lips were pink and full. Her smile was perfect, giving way to a dimple on one side. Flour dusted her chin and rolled-up sleeves, evidence of pie baking. Cody was dumbstruck. He couldn't take his eyes off her.

Millie said, "Uh, Cody? Say hello to Miss Penrose." She waited. "Cody?"

He cleared his throat, twice. "'Scuse me." He cleared it again. Lila stifled a giggle, her cheeks turning pinker. "Hullo, Miss Penrose," he finally said stiffly.

Silas looked at Cody, wondering what was ailing him. "You all right, son?"

Lila, in her sweet way, lightened the situation. "Just call me Lila." She smiled that perfect smile right at Cody and extended her hand. He held it a little long, his heart skipping a beat. *She's the purtiest thing I ever laid eyes on.*

After dinner, the men sat on the porch. Ike shared the story of how they discovered Cody's father out behind the chicken coop and how the men had prayed over his last words. Then he told about the earthquake and the way God woke him up in the night with a revelation to look in the cemetery.

Ike handed the map to Cody, with Silas looking over his shoulder. After they looked it over, Ike continued. "There was this here letter rolled up in it too."

Cody looked doubtful. "He never learnt ta read or write, my pa."

"Well, it says here that Father Francesca wrote it for him." He handed the letter to Cody, wondering if the boy could read or write himself. Thanks to Kate and Grace, he could.

Chapter 31

Church families loaned Silas and Cody sound horses and rifles for the journey, and they set out with Pastor Ike at daybreak for the rugged journey to Mission San Jose. Millie resigned herself to staying behind, knowing the three women would have a delightful time together but would miss out on the adventure. The fact that they carried guns and plenty of ammunition was not lost on her. The bits and pieces coming together spelled danger.

Cody reread part of the letter in his mind, puzzled:

> *I realize now in searching for gold, I've lost life's true treasure, my family. I pray to Jesus that my foolishness will somehow become a godsend to you, Cody. That my wasted past will create for you a blessed future. The maps combined hold the key to riches, but others lay claim to it. You must be very watchful. I pray you can forgive me. It breaks my heart, knowing the way I abandoned you. Even so, I love you.*

Finally, after two days of riding rocky high country, they spotted the mission below—or what was left of it. Many of the buildings had crumbled in the earthquake, but it appeared the church was mostly intact. Father Francesca and a few padres were still living there, determined to rebuild.

Pastor Ike made the introductions, although it was the first time he and the elderly priest had met in person. The old man said to Cody, "First, son, I want you to know your father atoned for his sins and accepted the gift of salvation. You can rest assured he was saved before he died. He was most sorry for his deserting you and Elizabeth, your mother. His prayer was that your life would be successful and that perhaps the gold would help."

Cody was bewildered by all this. The last time he'd seen his father, he was stupid drunk, passed out in a dirt alley. The part about gold finally sunk in. "So yer sayin' he struck gold?"

"Yes, son, he did, and much of it has been hidden on these grounds for a number of years. But I must warn you, there are claim jumpers who are determined that it belongs to them. They tracked your father to the mission and have tried to intimidate us over the past several years. They believe I know where it is hidden. The truth is, I do not. Your father very cleverly created two maps, both needed, one to overlap the other. You have half, and I have the other. You must understand, however, that the earthquake happened after your father's death. The location may have significantly shifted."

By candlelight, they studied the two maps, holding them up to the light, matching up various points. By midnight, the four were exhausted. Father Francesca retired to his makeshift quarters while Silas, Cody, and Pastor Ike stretched out on their bedrolls on the old mission floor.

At daybreak, after coffee and sparse vittles, they set out, trying to follow the map, which was a long, drawn-out process. Father Francesca stayed behind, while the three saddled their horses, making sure their rifles were secured in scabbards and their six guns in their holsters.

The mission grounds were scattered over several hundred acres. The maps seemed to lead away from the rubble of the buildings into the rugged hills. They rode as far as they could, and then Cody left his horse with Silas and Ike and climbed the steep crags like a deer, until he was out of sight.

Silas was feeling nervous. "Cody?" his call echoed. "*Cody!*"

Ike tried to sound reassuring. "Could be he found a cave. Maybe he can't hear ya."

"I'm goin' up there."

Just as Silas stepped off his horse, a voice echoed from above. It wasn't Cody's.

"Drop your gun belts, boys. Throw yer rifles to the ground. *Do it now,* or the kid gets it." Cody's hands were tied behind his back. On each side of him an outlaw made sure he didn't go anywhere. "Ya forgot the gun on that paint there."

Ike was down off his horse, and he tossed Cody's rifle to the ground.

"Look out!" Cody shouted, which brought a gut punch that knocked him to his knees. Two more outlaws had come up behind Silas and Ike. Now they were not only unarmed, but also outnumbered—not a good development.

Lord, please get us outa this here predicament, Ike prayed silently, thinking of Esther. *Gold or no gold, spare us, Lord Jesus. Our women are expecting us ta come home.* Silas thought about Millie. Cody thought about Lila, though he'd been thinking about her most the time anyway.

———

The three sat on the ground, leaning against hard rock, hands tied behind their backs, a pistol pointed in their faces. The other outlaws had the map. They were clambering through the hills, sure they were getting close. What they didn't know was the *other* map was tucked in Ike's Bible, inside his saddlebag.

Cody squirmed, trying to get comfortable against the rocks.

"Sit still, kid," the guard said before taking a swig from his canteen. Silas, having once been the same kind of no-account, figured it was whiskey. Sure enough, their captor began slowing a bit; looking drowsy.

Cody continued fidgeting. He had retrieved the blade from his boot; his long fingers were working to cut his hands free. Without the slightest movement, he passed the knife to Silas. *Good boy, Cody.* Silas was experienced at cutting himself free, and when the guard took another swig, he slipped the blade to Ike.

It happened all at once. Ike bellowed, "Snake!" causing enough distraction for Cody to spring like a cat and kick the pistol out of the stunned captor's hand. They faced off. Cody was tall but scrawny compared to the big man. Cody put a knee in the man's belly then a left hook in his jaw. Then Cody took a hit to the side of his head that knocked him to the ground.

Silas swooped in for the knockout. One big blow right between the eyes put the man out cold.

Cody turned toward Ike. "Thanks for the ol' snake—" He was about to say "trick" when a blast that made all their ears ring reverberated. Ike held the smoking gun in both hands, still aimed at some point on the rocks beyond.

"Weren't no trick, son," Ike said calmly. Sure enough, like an old rope, a dead rattler lay limp on the rocks.

The mystery of the map was solved, at least in part. The half that Frank Walton hid in the cemetery behind Hillside Methodist led them from the mission to a very small cave in the hills. They discovered that the cave opened into a vast network of caverns and passageways, essentially an underground maze. That was the second map. The gold was stashed in the deepest possible crater; it would have never been found without that map.

They would need additional supplies and torches, and hopefully some reinforcements to guard the cave's entrance. Father Francesca kindly agreed to gather everything they needed and sent one of the padres to recruit assistance. "When we find it," Cody said with assurance, "we'll make a considerable donation to help ya rebuild this here mission." Silas nodded, placing his hand on Cody's shoulder. He was proud of his boy.

They waited a day, rested, and got their supplies in order for the challenge ahead. On the following morning before the sun was up, they readied their horses and loaded supplies on a borrowed pack mule. Father Francesca stood at the portico to bless them and to pray for the operation. "Well, I'll be," Ike said. "Look over yonder, boys."

Coming over the hill was a small army of *vaqueros*, twenty-three in all. They lined their horses up facing Silas, Cody, and Ike. Each man wore a sombrero and carried a rifle. Father Francesca, who had stopped in the middle of his prayer, continued, "And thanks be to God Almighty for these reinforcements."

Chapter 32

Silas barely made it through the narrow opening of the cave. The three had removed their gun belts and excess clothing to squeeze through. Right inside, however, it opened into a huge space, the hub to a dozen passageways. With torches lit, they studied the map and agreed on the direction to take. It was slow going, dark and damp. Every now and then, their boots slipped in crumbling rock. The map had warned of dangerous footing on the edge of an underground hole, a deep one with water at the bottom.

"Somethin' ain't right here, boys," Silas's voice echoed. "Maybe we should go back to that last fork and go the other way."

Ike squinted to see the map. "I dunno. This seems right on one hand, but I confess to bein' disoriented."

The two men were hunched over the map, not realizing Cody had kept going. "We been at this a few hours, seems we should—" Somewhere up ahead came the sound of rocks crashing, then Cody's echoing cry for help, then his voice disappearing as if he had fallen in a pit. Silas and Ike moved clumsily as fast as possible toward the sound.

"*Cody?*" Silas was panic-stricken. "Cody?" Can you hear me, son?"

Faintly, as if Cody were a million miles away, they heard, "Be careful, Pa. There's a big hole. I'm on a ledge just above water. Got a rope up there?" With torches held into the chasm as far as possible, they couldn't see the boy, but by his voice they knew he was beyond the twelve feet of rope they had with them.

Silas lay on his belly, talking into total blackness, trying to keep Cody alert. *What's takin' so long?*

Ike had gone for help from the cavalry of Spaniards. He ran like a young man, praying all the way. Finally, he saw daylight, the opening of the cave. It dawned on him that they wouldn't understand his English, but he blurted out anyway, "We need help! The boy has fallen into a very deep hole. Ropes. We need ropes!" At first they stared at him. Then one of the old Spaniards shouted orders in his native tongue. Within seconds, three vaqueros, two with torches and the third with a long rope, rushed forward.

Cody had landed on a ledge two feet wide at best, and he lay there barely conscious from lack of oxygen. "Keep talking to me, son. Cody? Son? I love ya, son. We got a lot ahead of us. You an' me an' Millie. Cody?"

"I—hear—" Cody gasped. He was so very tired. *God, I don't deserve Your help. I been nothin' but trouble my whole life. I'm sorry, God. Please help me—please—*

There was a commotion above, strange lingo echoing far away. The three Spaniards launched into action like they rescued someone every day. In the torchlight, they quickly fashioned a harness from strong rope, leaving a length attached to it. The whole thing was connected to an additional eighty feet. A young vaquero about Cody's size speedily slipped into the harness and pulled it taught. The other two, with the help of Silas and Ike, lowered him quickly. A torch in his hand, he eventually spotted Cody and with nimble feet lowered himself within reach.

Once the two were securely tied together, the young man signaled his *compadres* and, with inch-by-inch progress, brought them to the top. Silas gathered Cody, in a state of collapse, into his strong arms.

Cody could barely speak, but his words were not lost on the odd lot gathered there. "Thank you—God."

It took another day and a half, but they did find the gold. They had camped two nights, growing in comradery with their new friends, sharing beans and bacon and laughter even though they didn't speak the same language. Cody recovered and was enjoying the campfire and the starlit sky, but he remained quiet and contemplative after his rescue.

To their surprise, when their mission was finally finished and they were making their way for the last time out of the cave, there sat the four phony claim jumpers, bound and gagged. The reinforcements provided by Father Francesca turned out to be twenty-three gifts from God.

———

The three women had pieced and quilted an entire quilt and were working on a small one for Grace and Sam's baby. Millie was at her wit's end. "It's been ten days," she cried. "They should have been back by now."

"And we have prayed all ten, Millie dear," Esther said with a calm she didn't quite feel. "I trust the Lord to bring them back safely."

"Me too!" exclaimed Lila. Somehow she knew Cody would be back.

Several church families had stopped by to check on the ladies and bring an occasional fruit pie or plate of cookies. Millie truly enjoyed the growing friendship the three shared, but over the past few days her nerves had been on edge with worry.

That evening, as they tidied up after supper, Lila shouted from the porch, "They're back! The men are home."

"Praise God!" Millie and Esther exclaimed in unison. They ran for the porch, getting momentarily stuck trying to get through the door at the same time. The men looked beat, like they had lost weight; unshaven and dirty. But Millie ran into Silas's waiting embrace, as well as Esther into Ike's, which left Lila and Cody looking at each other. Cody went ahead and hugged her awkwardly, and Lila hugged back.

They had decided not to mention Cody's near-death episode, but Millie sensed a change in the boy—a mellowing. He was quiet, preoccupied much of the time. In spite of that, after two days of recuperating, Cody announced, "Today Miss Millie will see the ocean."

Millie was touched that, after all that had happened, he remembered. "I can't wait. And please come with us," she insisted of the Penroses.

Silas chimed in, "We shore would be tickled ta have y'all with us."

Cody added, "Already rented a horse and buggy for six."

"That's a mighty big expense, son," Ike said.

Cody chuckled. "You forget? I got 'nuff gold in the bank ta buy the thing." Everybody laughed.

The weather was perfect: sunshine, no fog. Millie and Lila made sandwiches from fresh bread, compliments of Ursula, and leftover ham. While Esther's berry cobbler was in the oven, she assembled a basket of utensils and tin cups, a jug of sweet tea, and gathered blankets. They were bursting with excitement.

Cody, with permission, shared with the others Millie's crazy dream of seeing the ocean. Millie laughed at the thought. "Remember, Cody? How we sat out there by the wood shed drinkin' coffee, talkin'?"

He laughed too. "I'll never forget it, ma'am."

Millie continued, "And what about *your* dream, Cody? Did ya ever figure it out?"

"I'm thinkin' on it. Still thinkin' on it." He shot a glance at Lila. *I got me a few ideas all right.*

They were nearly there. Silas instructed his wife, "Now close your eyes, Millie."

"Yeah," echoed Cody, "close 'em till we say." Ike pulled the wagon to a rocky spot just above the beach. "Now!"

Millie opened her eyes. "Oh my! Oh my goodness!" Silas helped her down from the buggy. The breeze off the magnificent Pacific blew her hair loose. They made their way down through the rocks to the beach, Millie giggling like a girl. Truth be told, all of them were as excited as kids.

Cody and Lila followed the grownups, hauling the picnic basket and blankets. "This is wonderful, Cody," Lila said sweetly. Her bonnet had blown back, so strands of auburn curls flew in every direction. Cody could not quit stealing glances at her.

"It *is* wonderful," he said.

"I sure was glad when you—when all of you—made it back. I prayed for you every day, Cody."

"For me?" He couldn't believe it.

"Well, I prayed for all of you but something tugged on me to pray extra for you."

The blankets were spread, but Millie couldn't sit. She walked right to the surf, arms open wide. "Lord God! You are magnificent. Oh my." She stood there mesmerized, the wind blowing her skirts and her hair, tears streaming.

Cody slipped up beside her. "Is it just like I said?"

"Oh yes, and even more. It's endless, just like you said. So like God's love, Cody. Endless! I can't see the edges in any direction." She pulled him into a hug. "Thank ya, Cody. You kept your word. You made my dream come true. Thank ya, son. Thank ya. I'll never forget this moment."

Chapter 33

After lunch, Cody and Lila took a walk on the beach, picking up shells and pretty pebbles, and talking. "Wanta get your feet wet?" Cody asked with a smile. But then he wanted to take it back, thinking it might not be proper, especially now that they were a good distance from the adults. Nevertheless Lila sat in the sand and unlaced her boots. Cody did likewise, and they cautiously stepped into the foamy shore.

"Oooh, it's so cold!" Lila squealed. She picked up her skirts a bit, laughing as salt water splashed her legs. Cody was laughing just because she was. When their feet became numb and started turning a little blue, they decided to sit in the sun for a spell before walking back. They chatted about nothing special, leaning back on their elbows, watching the ocean.

Out of the blue, Cody sat up, still facing straight ahead. "Somethin' happened to me when I was on the ledge."

She looked at him, puzzled. "What ledge, Cody?"

"Oh." Cody hesitated. "Please don't tell Millie. We didn't intend the women find out."

"What happened? I won't say a word."

Cody described their trek in the cave, how unreal it was—and scary. "I got ahead of Silas and your pa somehow, but I had a torch and thought I could see. My foot slipped, rocks crumbled, and all of a sudden I was fallin' into a deep pit. It seemed bottomless. Somehow I landed on a ledge. Rocks flew past me and plunked into water deep down."

Lila turned to face him, her arms hugging her knees. "Oh, Cody. You could have died down there! How did you ever get out?"

Cody described the whole rescue mission and the Spaniards risking their own lives. "When I was down there, I couldn't stay awake. No oxygen. But Silas kept shoutin' down to me, tryin' to keep me talkin'. The ledge was only this wide." He held his hands apart about fifteen inches. "I confess I'm not much of the praying type, but I prayed. I ain't been a good soul, Lila. It was a long shot, me prayin'. But I felt real sorry for all I done wrong and told God so."

Tears spilled from Lila's hazel eyes; she was barely breathing. Cody continued. "It happened right then. The brightest light I ever seen filled up that hole. It seemed I was floatin', lookin' down at myself layin' there." He looked at her then. "You think I'm crazy, Lila?"

She sniffed. "No, Cody, I don't think you're crazy a bit. I think you saw God."

It felt good, telling Lila what had happened in the cave. Cody kept talking as they leisurely strolled back toward their families. "The whole thing is so perplexing. My pa never wanted a thing ta do with me, and then he leaves me all his gold." Cody told of his childhood, of being abandoned, left to make it on his own at the age of nine, and how he was in trouble most the time; scared the rest.

Lila reached for his hand. He gladly took hers. "My parents didn't want me either." She said it so quietly, he didn't think he heard right.

"Anyone can see you're their pride and joy. Your ma and pa love you better than anything!"

She hesitated a bit and said, "They're not my real parents, Cody. I was left on the back porch, a newborn baby. Right next to a bushel of apples."

It was time for the train to depart. Leaving Lila Penrose felt awful. "Will ya write me, Lila?"

"Of course, Cody. Will you write me too?" He held her gaze. They were lost to the crowd around them: the Mitchells and Penroses sharing their own good-byes. The two families had become attached, like they'd known each other a lifetime.

Lila's eyes pooled. So did Cody's. Her beautiful face was inches from his. Cody gently tugged on a ringlet of her sweet-smelling hair. He took a deep breath then kissed her quickly on the lips.

———

After the train jerked to a start, Silas and Millie dozed, leaving Cody to his thoughts. About an hour had passed, when Millie woke up, stretched, and reached for the lunch Esther had packed. The trip heading east seemed much more comfortable and enjoyable. Millie discovered a note tucked in the lunch basket.

The Penrose family is grateful to God for our newly formed friendship with the Mitchell family. All three of you blessed us in so many ways. We are praying about us taking a trip to Thatcher Springs next summer. Until then, you three, Silas, Millie, and Cody, will be in our hearts and prayers.

God bless you, Ike, Esther, and Lila Jane

Silas looked up at Cody. "Your sweet on 'er, ain't ya, son?"

Cody took a bite of sandwich and chewed it slowly, thinking. He swallowed and took a swig of cider. "I'm aimin' ta marry her, Pa."

Millie choked on a cookie. Silas just smiled, taking it lightly. Something else had his attention. "Ya know, Cody, that's the second time here lately y'all called me Pa. Does that mean you're agreein' ta be our legal son?"

Cody chuckled, reaching for a cookie. Millie leaned forward, her blue eyes big with anticipation. "Reckon it does," said Cody. "And long as I'm confessin' everything, when we get home, I wanta be baptized.

Chapter 34

Gus Carter was a twenty-six-year-old widower. His beloved Addie was only eighteen when she died, caught in the crossfire during a bank robbery. She had told Gus a few days earlier she was carrying their first baby. They were ecstatic.

The bad guys got away, but Gus relentlessly pursued them, filled with revenge. He was driven to find the killer and even the score. He was no longer the fun-loving, good-natured guy he had once been. He quit his family and friends—and quit God. That was four years ago.

Tom, his older brother, had tried to convince him to make a change. "Go out west with me, Gus. The air is fresh; the people are good folks. I know a place we can get work. What d'ya say, brother?"

Missouri held nothing for either one, but Gus felt a need to stay close to Addie's grave. He thought he'd get a lead on the one that killed her. The only thing that got him thinking about leaving was overhearing that the same band of robbers had hit a bank in Cheyenne. He thought he could track them from there. Eventually he ended up in Thatcher Springs, doing what he knew: blacksmithing.

The people there were nice, and the food was good—Tom being a skilled cook and the ladies baking fine pastries. For some reason, the youngsters took to him, especially little Ruthie K. She wanted to sit by him whenever the Reeds came up for dinner. No one cracked the hard surface of Gus's heart quite like Ruthie.

The whole population of Thatcher Springs set out early one morning to whitewash the inn, a surprise for Millie upon her return from California. Everyone pitched in, young and old alike. Josh, Joe, and the Montague boys made a contest out of it, with two up on a rickety scaffold and two on the ground. Jake and Ruthie wanted to help "Uncle Gus." Jake worked from Gus's big bucket and Ruthie from her own little pail. She carefully painted on the low boards, her father checking on her periodically.

"Be careful, Ruthie," Max instructed. "Are these two a trouble to ya, Gus?"

"No trouble at all. They're doin' a fine job, Max," Gus said with a wink. He felt a comfort being with the children. They accepted him with no demands. Eating together, painting together—they just liked being with him.

Things were going fine until Ruthie backed up to admire her work and stumbled on uneven ground. The little bucket dumped its contents in the lap of her calico pinafore. "Uh oh."

Gus and Jake turned at the sound. "Ruthie K!" Jake exclaimed. "You wrecked your dress. You're really gonna catch it."

Her lower lip shot out and eyebrows furrowed. She started toward Gus, reaching her arms out to him. "Oh, Unco Bus," she cried. "Rufie dunna tetch it." He scooped her up, patting her gently on the back as she sobbed into his neck.

"It's okay, little one. It's okay. It was an accident. Your ma and pa will understand." A fleeting ache tugged at his heart for his own child, the one he would never know.

She looked up at his face, trying hard to stop crying. "Am I dunna det a whuppin'?"

"No, sweetheart. It was just a little mishap." He kept her in his arms and ruffled Jake's hair. "C'mon, you two, we need ta take us a cookie break."

"I wuv you, Unco Bus."

He squeezed her tighter, unable to answer for the lump in his throat. *I love you too, Ruthie K.*

—————

Cody tucked the letter deep in his vest pocket, planning to wait until dinner break to slip out back and read it. His heart beat with anticipation, his energy increased for the job at hand: splitting wood.

Finally, he was alone, sitting in the hayloft. He carefully tore the letter open. It was written on delicate stationary. The fragrance of her soap escaped the opened envelope. He closed his eyes, thinking of her beautiful eyes, the way her hair bounced with every step, the way she gently took his hand, her pretty little feet dancing in the surf. He longed for the day he would see her again.

April 16, 1873

Dear Cody,

It was a wonderful blessing to receive your letter. I have been thinking about you too, especially our walking and talking on the beach. God seems to be doing so much in your life, Cody. He brought you out of that awful pit (read Psalms 40:2). He must have great plans for your life. I can't help but wonder how He will use you in His kingdom.

What happy news that Silas and Millie are now your legal parents. Their love for you was evident during the time you all were here. And now I'm praying that I will be coming there with my parents to Thatcher Springs. Papa thinks maybe September.

Things have been going well here, except for one mishap. After surviving the big earthquake, my violin was crushed by a rambunctious horse! I'm grateful no one was hurt, but I surely miss my violin. Papa wants me to sing in church next Sunday, but I think I may wake up that day with a fever. Haha.

I will keep you in my prayers, Cody, and hope you will pray for me too.

Lila

That night Cody opened Henry's old Bible and read Psalm 40:2. "He brought me up also out of a horrible pit, out of the miry clay, and set my feet upon a rock, and established my goings." He read it again. And again. Lila was right. God was doing something in his life. He thought back about the days when he had nobody, when no one cared a whit about him. Back then he had been full of anger, never caring how much trouble he got into. He was not once the least bit concerned that he stole from others.

Then Silas came into his life, bringing Millie, Max and Kate, Josh and Joe, Grace and Sam, and all the others. And if that weren't enough, there was Lila Penrose. *Lord, You sure did pull me out of that miry pit, in more ways than one. It's almost impossible to understand how You took a loser like me and an outlaw like Silas and brought us together. And him holdin' up that stagecoach so long ago and everything that happened since then. You have ta be real. I thought 'I'm gonna die' in that black hole, Lord, but You saved me. You saved me. I owe You, God. I'm gonna do right by You. That's a promise.*

———

Pastor Ike went to town once a week to pick up the mail and whatever supplies Esther might need. Most of the time, Lila stayed home with her mother, but hoping there might be a letter from Cody, she asked if she could go along with her father on that sunny day.

There was a letter, much to her delight. She stuffed it in her pocket so she could read it in private.

Ike sent her to the Mercantile next door, while he had a cup of coffee with Clyde at the bakery. "You can collect this here list a things," he told her. "And get yourself a peppermint stick. Maybe get me one too, sweetheart." He watched her walk happily down the boardwalk, thinking to himself, *what an angel of a daughter God has given me.*

She did her shopping and left the bundle of goods with Mr. Callahan, the proprietor of the Mercantile. Then she sat on the porch bench, enjoying her peppermint stick, taking in the sights, waiting for her father. Her heart beat a little faster than usual as she thought about Cody's letter.

The dirt road through town seemed extra busy that day. Horse-drawn wagons and buggies, and a number of single riders were going in both directions, stirring up the dust. She waved and called out a friendly hello to those she knew, mostly from church.

Beyond the street and down a bit was the saloon. The sound of honky-tonk piano music coming from that direction drew her attention. Men were coming and going, and the walk out front was busy with passersby. Suddenly, Lila sat up straight. *There she is.* A woman in the shadows was looking right at her. Lila had seen her one other time, when the woman's bonnet had blown back, exposing thick red curls like her own. The woman darted inside. There was something about her that put a twang in Lila's belly. *Why is she looking at me?*

Ike met with Clyde for more than the usual chitchat. He was troubled and wanted to get Clyde's thoughts on a certain matter. "I got an uneasy feelin', Clyde. Somethin's goin' on. When Lila's horse acted up the other day and her cinch busted, it wasn't a accident. Somebody cut the leather."

Clyde held his coffee midway to his mouth, a shocked look on his face. "Ya mean ta say some lowdown varmint is tryin' ta harm Lila?"

Ike shook his head. "I don't know what ta think, but I'm keepin' a close watch on her."

So that's why he picked the winder seat, Clyde thought.

"Keep it to yourself for now, brother," Ike concluded. "And pray about it, if ya would."

Lila thought Ike was taking an awful long time, and she couldn't wait another minute. Carefully, she tore open the envelope and began to read Cody's letter. She smiled and read it again. Twice.

May 5, *1873*

Dear Lila,

I'm sure sorry to hear about your violin, but if your voice is anything like the rest of you, it must be real pretty. You are right about God workin on me. So much has happened. I don't mean the gold. Hardly ever think of it, to tell the truth. But I do think about you Lila. Just waitin for you to get here, so I can show you around and we can talk. This letter writin ain't near as good as bein with you, like when we walked on the beach.

I read the Bible verse you gave me. That was me in that pit all right and I been readin more. Thank you for prayin for me. I pray for you every time I think of you, which is a lot. It seems forever until I see you again.

Give my best wishes to your ma and pa.

Yours truly, Cody

Chapter 35

Pearl had taken on serving duties in the dining room and did so with flair. In the dark-blue uniform and starched white apron that Millie required, she looked like a different person than when she and her sisters had arrived in colorful fancy duds that long-ago day. Now with no makeup and her dark hair pulled back into a neat twist, she was lovely. In fact, for the first time, Gus noticed her when she poured his coffee and sweetly offered a plate of warm biscuits, butter, and jam.

"Thank ya, ma'am. And I'd like ta order a hot chocolate. I'm expectin' a guest any minute."

When Pearl returned with the steaming chocolate, there sat Ruthie K right next to Gus. "Auntie Pool!"

Pearl picked her up from the big chair and hugged her close. "You know what, Ruthie K? I haven't seen you for two days. I *missed* you."

"I missed you too, Auntie Pool. Wanta have coffee wiff me an' Unco Bus?"

Pearl laughed and set the Ruthie back down in her chair. "Well, maybe after I get everyone served." She glanced at Gus, who seemed to be staring at her.

He stammered, "Uh, sure. Be pleased ta have ya join us—Auntie Pool."

A little blush colored her cheeks. "Why thank you, Unco Bus."

———

Ever since Sammy had arrived five months before, Silas said of Millie, "She's gone daffy." Grace and Sam's baby boy was remarkably beautiful, with his papa's dark skin, Grace's blue eyes, and gobs of black hair sticking out in every direction. Millie adored all her "babies," but something was special about Sammy.

In fact, she even invited everyone to a shindig in celebration of his first tooth. The men were snickering and giving Silas a bad time, but they couldn't deny the tantalizing aromas coming from the kitchen all afternoon. Everybody loved Millie's parties, no matter the reason.

After supper, warm chocolate apple cake was served, along with a little bowl of pudding for Sammy. Tom tuned up his banjo and played it flawlessly. He played his mouth harp at the same time; a contraption anchored to his shoulders held it. Cody played the gutbucket.

Max led Kate out to the dance floor to get things rolling, and before long everyone joined in, even the toddlers. Of course, Gus couldn't resist when Ruthie dragged him out in the middle of the floor, holding his hands and looking up at him sweetly. Tom broke into a lively jig, which sent Ruthie into a fit of giggles. Gus didn't dance like everybody else, but he felt relaxed and enjoyed the antics of his dance partner.

She stopped midstride. "You wanta cool dwink, Unco Bus?"

"That sounds good, Ruthie. Lead the way."

Pearl was the only one not dancing, but she felt happy to serve everyone coffee and cider. Since living in Thatcher Springs, so much had changed. She had grown close to the Lord, and though she had always pictured herself married to a man of position, living a high lifestyle, lately she'd been thinking of the mission field. The circuit preacher had left some leaflets about missionaries needed in China, and in some cases women were accepted. *Wherever you lead me, Lord, I will follow.*

Her thoughts were interrupted with a tugging on her gown. "Auntie Pool?"

Gus stood awkwardly, holding Ruthie's hand. He shifted from one foot to the other, then exclaimed, "Uh, we worked up a powerful thirst out there."

"Well, y'all came to the right place," Pearl said, smiling up at Gus. Their eyes held a moment. Then Pearl poured two cups of cider, a big one and a small one. "Looks like you two were having fun."

Ruthie gulped down her cider with one hand, while still holding onto Gus. She reached for Pearl's hand and then as if it was expected, put their two hands together. "You dance with Unco Bus now. Rufie tired."

Pearl tried to pull away, but not too hard. Gus didn't let go. She looked down at her toes, her cheeks warming. Gus was blushing too. Tom began a waltz, and Ruthie said, "Go on. I can do coffee and juice."

Slowly they walked onto the floor. Gus placed his hand on the small of her back and led her in waltzing around the room. He was amazed he could remember how and even more amazed that he was enjoying the feel of this beautiful woman in his arms.

After that, Gus and Pearl were often together, riding or walking in the evening, sitting on the porch, talking, sometimes late into the night. Gus told her about his shattered dreams when Addie was killed, about the vengefulness he still harbored.

Pearl shared how her life had changed since coming to Thatcher Springs, how the Lord had done the changing. "Truth be told, I was spoiled rotten," she said. "Full of anger and jealousy, selfishness." Gus looked at her, puzzled. He had come to know her as sweet and humble, a lot like Kate. "I had to lay it down, Gus. Walk away from my old life. I know it's not easy, but I'm gonna pray for you—pray that you will trust God, pray that He gives you strength to let it go."

Gus was humbled and touched. "Nobody's prayed for me in a long time, Pearl. I thank ya."

———

Sunday after church and dinner, Gus hopped up from the table and began helping Pearl and the other ladies clear the tables. "Well, thank you, sir," Pearl exclaimed with a shy smile.

"I was just thinkin' if I helped out a bit you could get away sooner." He looked hopeful.

"Get away and do what?" She waited, wondering what he had in mind.

"Uh, well—go fishin'?"

She hadn't been fishing since she was twelve. "That sounds like a fine idea. I'll be ready in thirty minutes."

Chapter 36

May22, 1873

Dear Cody,

Thank you for writing me and praying for me too. I can hardly wait to come out there and see you and meet the rest of your family. It's wonderful you are reading God's Word. It will bless you more than you can imagine.

How are things going for you otherwise? Have the snows melted? It has been mostly raining here, with some signs of spring ever so often. Mama just walked in and says hello.

You are a wonderful person, Cody. I'm thankful to God for you, and that we met. It seems like forever until September. I am anxious to share some things with you. Just be praying.

Your friend,
Lila

For the third time in as many weeks, Lila rode into town with her father and was delighted to find another letter from Cody in the mail, especially after coming up empty the week before. It had become routine for Ike to meet up with Clyde and send Lila next door to the Mercantile. He could lean against the window and see her feet crossed as she sat on the bench. He kept a close watch on her.

"I just got a gut feelin', Clyde. Nothin's happened since the horse wreck, but somethin's not right. I'm thinkin' this has ta do with the gold."

Clyde rubbed his scruffy jaw. "The Walton kid's gold? Ain't it in the bank?"

"Well, sure it is. I dunno. It's just a feelin', I guess." The waitress poured more coffee. When Ike looked back out the window, he didn't see Lila's feet. *Hmm. She must've gone back in the store.*

But unease gripped him. "Be back in a minute, Clyde." He jumped up so fast, the chair fell, and coffee splashed on the table.

Ike rushed into the Mercantile, his eyes searching as he called out to Ben Callahan. "Ben, have ya seen Lila? Did she come back in?"

Ben leaned over the counter, looking out the front window. "She's been right there on the bench, Pastor Ike. Hasn't been five minutes since I saw her sittin' right there."

Ike tore back out, panic rising in his chest. "Lila? *Lila!*" He walked briskly down the steps at the end of the porch, across the alley, opening the doors of each establishment he passed, calling her name.

Clyde caught up to him. "Maybe she got a notion to look in the dressmaker shop. Probably somethin' like that, Ike."

"I don't think so, brother. You keep goin' this way, and I'll backtrack and go past the bakery and on down the other way. And Clyde? Pray with everything ya got."

Ike walked back the way he'd come, but with more intention. He stopped at the alley. *Someone could have lured her to this alley and took her out the back way.* Ike marched down the dirt alley, hand on his holster. *Keep her safe, Lord. Keep my baby girl safe.*

Cody looked up from his fence mending to see a cloud of dust roaring their way. He took off his hat, marveling at Warrior, who was moving faster than ever. Roy pulled Warrior to a quick stop and jumped off, which was not usual. In fact, Cody realized it was two days before his regular schedule. Roy was leading the horse, jogging toward Cody, who began to feel something was wrong. Cody headed toward him, and when they met, Roy handed him a letter.

Trying to catch his breath, Roy blurted out, "It's urgent! From a preacher in Frisco. Penrose." Without hesitation, Cody ripped it open.

Cody, you must come at once. Lila is being held hostage for ransom. Don't know where they took her. We think it's those no-account varmints that laid claim to your gold. Clyde found out they got outa jail. A ransom note was slid under the church door and Lila, in her own hand, wrote she was all right. Pray for her and us and please come quick.

Millie couldn't calm the boy when he burst into the kitchen with the letter. "I've gotta go now! Max shod my horse this mornin'. Just need some grub and—"

"Cody, dear, sit for a minute."

Right then Silas walked in. "Roy told me, son. Let's figure a plan."

Though Cody had just sat down, he jumped up. "What's wrong with you people? Lila's in terrible danger. I *gotta go!*"

Silas put a hand on his shoulder. "I understand, Cody, but you can't run a horse all the way to the West Coast. It took three riders to get that letter here."

Millie chimed in, "You could take the train and transport Stormy in the stock car, at least halfway."

Cody sucked in a breath and sat again. The three discussed options over hot coffee and decided together, like a family, that Cody would ride his horse to a rail town in Utah and take the train from there. He would feel better just getting on that horse.

Millie reached for Silas's and Cody's hands. "Well, we shoulda done it first off, but let's pray." Cody had been praying all right—praying like sixty for his sweet Lila. He had never felt so helpless in his life. *Please, Lord, keep her safe. Don't let her be afraid.* Somehow he knew Lila wouldn't be afraid. Her faith ran deep—too deep to be afraid. A peaceful feeling washed over him.

———

They had her bound and gagged in a sparse, dingy room with wallpaper peeling off the walls and meager furnishings in disrepair. Lila knew she was above the saloon from the sounds wafting upstairs: honky-tonk piano, bursts of laughter, men's voices.

She had left her bench at the Mercantile that day to help an old woman with a shawl over her head. But the old woman turned out to be a man. He clamped a hand on her mouth and packed her down the alley to a waiting wagon. She struggled against the odds, as another man helped. They tied her wrists together behind her back. Roughly they crammed her in the back of the wagon, between sacks of potatoes, and threw the shawl over her.

Now there she sat in that darkened, creepy room, thinking of her parents and how frantically they would be looking for her. She closed her eyes, recalling verses from the Bible and words to hymns she knew so well. *I know you are with me, Lord. I am not afraid.* She remembered Cody's unopened letter, still in her pocket. It gave her a flicker of courage.

———

Cody met up with Ike in town. Two more ransom notes had appeared at the church, which was now heavily guarded, at least as much as Clyde and Jesse could stay awake. Their wives settled in with Esther, trying to keep her optimistic and busy. She was beside herself with fear that she'd never see her girl again.

Ike spoke in hushed tones as he and Cody sat at the bakery—at the same table Ike had sat at with Clyde when Lila disappeared. Ike said, "The kidnappers made it sound like they took her far off up in the hills. But I got a notion she could be right here in town." For the hundredth time, it seemed, he told Cody everything he could recall about that day. "They're demanding $5,000 for Lila's return."

Lila had no idea how much time had gone by, but she did know she was hungry and getting cold—uncomfortable, to say the least. *The Lord is my strength. My trust is in You, Lord. I am not afraid.*

The door creaked open, casting a shaft of smoky light across the room, and then closed again quickly. Lila could not see who entered. A lamp flickered to life on the other side of the room, revealing a woman, her face in the shadows. Her skirts rustled as she quickly stepped over to Lila. In barely a whisper, she said, "I brought you some vittles, but you must keep quiet when I remove the gag. You gonna be quiet?" Lila nodded. "Jeb and Sonny would kill me if they knew that I brung food from the kitchen." When the woman left, she didn't put the gag back in Lila's mouth.

Chapter 37

The next day, the woman came earlier; light was still coming through the window. Lila recognized her. It was the woman that had watched her from a distance—the one with red curls. Up close, she looked younger than she had, but dark circles under her eyes and pale skin spoke of a hard life.

"I'm gonna untie your hands, Lila, but if the men come, you put 'em back behind ya. D'ya hear?"

Lila nodded. "How'd ya know my name?" The red-haired woman didn't say anything. Lila stretched her aching arms, so relieved to be untied, her eyes never leaving the woman.

"Here's a clean cloth and a pan of water. Wash your face; you'll feel better."

"Thank you, Miss—" The woman didn't answer. Lila risked asking, "What is your name?"

The woman stammered, "Kitty."

"Thank you, Miss Kitty."

Kitty returned again that evening with a dinner of bacon, beans, and a stale biscuit. She poured hot coffee for both of them and then sat on the floor facing Lila, leaning against the bed. "You've become a very beautiful young woman, Lila." She spoke with tenderness, giving Lila confidence.

"What is it they want, Kitty? Why am I held hostage?"

Kitty stood, went to the window, and pulled the curtain back slightly. The horses were still gone. Jeb and Sonny had taken off to deliver another note—one with a deadline. They told Kitty they would circle around and come in behind the church building, and that she was to keep a close eye on the girl.

"They say the Walton kid's gold belongs to them. They don't aim ta harm ya, Lila. Soon as they get the gold, they'll let ya go."

Lila shook her head in disbelief. "My family must be worried sick," she said, mostly to herself. "And Cody has no idea all this is happening." Without a thought of Kitty sitting there, Lila bowed her head and prayed aloud, "Lord Jesus, please keep my parents safe. Surround them with your angels. May they trust you, Lord, and be at peace in the midst of this trouble. Protect me too, Lord. And Miss Kitty."

It was nearly dark. Cody saw the curtain move, and in that split second he spotted Lila. Ike had combed the entire city over and over during the week since she went missing, but Cody knew the town like the back of his hand. He had climbed on the roof of the CJ Stanton Law Offices, a tall building giving a view into second-floor windows of several establishments across the road.

Quick as a cat, he leaped across to the next building, dropped into the alley, and crept in the shadows until he was across the road and behind the saloon. There was no way to scale the back side of the saloon. Next door, in the building that housed the barber and bathhouse, was a rickety staircase to the second floor. From the top of that building, he thought he might be able to sling his rope to the saloon's chimney and pull himself onto the roof.

Lila and Kitty were in deep conversation after the prayer. Kitty admitted two reasons for her part in the hostage taking. The first was that Jeb and Sonny promised to give her three hundred dollars of the ransom money. "That kinda money will get me out of this rotten town, out of the State of California. Three hundred bucks will give me a chance to start over somewhere else." Tears brimmed in her eyes when she said it.

"And what's the other reason?" Lila asked.

Kitty bit her lower lip, hesitating. "I wanted to protect you, Lila." There was a long silence.

Lila looked decisively at the woman sitting across from her. "Are you my birthmother, Kitty?" Deep inside, she'd known it all along. Looking at Kitty was like looking in a faded mirror; she was an older version of herself.

Kitty swallowed hard, tears now spilling over. She buried her head in her hands. Lila sat staring, stunned with the truth of it. "I was so young. No means to care for a child. Ever'body said the preacher was a good man and had a fine wife." Lila wanted to comfort her, to embrace her, but she couldn't move.

Suddenly, both women looked up at the sound of men's voices outside the door. Neither could move in time. Sonny kicked the door open. "What in tarnation is goin' on, Kitty?" He roughly yanked her to her feet.

Jeb grabbed Lila, seeing she was untied, and wrenched her hands behind her back. "This ain't no tea party, little lady," he hollered.

"Let her be, Jeb. She ain't gonna run. She knows about the ransom money."

Sonny slapped Kitty so hard she fell to the floor.

Lila gasped. Though she was about the sweetest thing in God's creation, being a witness to that kind of brutality unleashed something inside her. She jabbed Jeb with an elbow to the belly and walked right up to Sonny, hands on hips. She stabbed a finger into his chest as she said, "You are one lowdown skunk to hit a woman. I sure wouldn't wanta be in your boots on Judgment Day!"

At the sound of breaking glass, they all hunkered down. Jeb and Sonny drew their pistols; Kitty worked her way over to Lila and took her hand. A voice shouted through the broken window. Cody's voice. "Drop your guns! Now!" Cody had a rifle in his left hand, a pistol in his right.

It took Jeb and Sonny a little too long to submit. Cody fired a shot into the wall behind them, and their pistols fell to the floor. Kitty grabbed one, Lila the other.

Jeb was about to reach for the derringer in his boot when the door burst open, revealing Cody's posse. Ike, Clyde, and Jesse stormed in with guns drawn. Ike could only run to his daughter. "Papa! Oh, Papa, I knew you'd come." She looked over Ike's shoulder, locking eyes with Cody. "I knew you'd come," she said again.

The sheriff hauled off Jeb and Sonny, swearing he'd see them rot in San Quentin. Ike walked over to Cody and drew him into a bear hug. "You're one tough feller, Cody Walton. I thank ya—" He choked up and couldn't finish.

"Well, sir, I'm just thankful to God we found her." He looked across the room at Lila. "And I might add, she's a plucky little thing."

Ike took a deep breath. "Well then, let's go home. Ma's probably faint with fear."

Lila turned to Kitty. "Come home with us, Kitty." Ike looked taken back, and so did Kitty. "Just for a few days' rest." Ike shook his head. *My daughter is a better Christian than I am.* He smiled at Kitty. "By all means, ma'am. Esther's fine cookin' will do ya a world a good."

The next day was Sunday. With all the goings on, Ike hadn't prepared a sermon to preach, but he sure did have a message. Word got out about Lila getting rescued, and by the time the church service ended, the grounds were filled with tables of food in celebration. Lila and Cody got most of the attention, and Kitty was amazed at how kindhearted all of them were to her. After a good meal and a hot bath the night before and now dressed in a borrowed gown, she looked like a different person. Pretty. But deep inside, she knew they all recognized the truth. She was a saloon girl. And yet they showered her with kindness.

In the late afternoon, Cody finally got the chance to be with Lila alone. They walked up the hill behind the churchyard, walking without speaking. All at once they turned to face each other. "Lila," Cody said, right when she said, "Cody." They laughed shyly then Cody cupped her face in his hands, looking deeply into her eyes.

"Lila, I couldn't bear it if anything happened to you. I think of you day and night. When I heard you'd been kidnapped, well, it made me crazy."

Lila's eyes pooled up. "Oh, Cody, you are always on my mind too. I just knew you'd come for me. You're my hero."

He drew her closer and kissed her forehead, her nose and, very tenderly, her lips. "I love you, Lila Penrose." He enveloped her in his strong arms. Lila didn't resist, but wrapped her arms around his neck. He kissed her again, fervently.

She kissed back and breathlessly whispered, "I love you too, Cody."

Chapter 38

Cody sent word back home that Lila was safe and that he planned to stay in San Francisco for another two weeks or so, in order to conduct some business. When he finally did get back to Thatcher Springs, everyone clamored to hear the story of Lila's rescue. As much as he hated leaving Lila, it felt good to be home.

At the late hour, Millie suggested Cody get a good night's sleep and everyone gather after supper the next evening to hear the whole story.

There was barely a dry eye in the room when Cody finished telling the rescue story. Everyone was especially touched by the part about Kitty being Lila's birthmother. Millie's tears were mostly for the pride she felt seeing Cody standing there, now a tall and very handsome young man.

"Before y'all turn in," Cody began, "I have some other things to share." He cleared his throat. "Not sure where ta begin." A little laughter relaxed the tension he was feeling. "I met with a lawyer in San Francisco, one that Pastor Ike recommended—about the gold and how I want to set it up. So, first off, I ordered a vault of the best quality. It'll be delivered here, and in the meantime, I'd like ta get your agreement to build a bank right here in Thatcher Springs."

The crowd cheered and laughed with excitement at the prospect. "Cuz," Cody went on, "you all are gonna need a place ta keep your money." They looked at each other, puzzled.

Silas laughed. "My money don't even fill up a pickle jar."

Cody continued. "You people, every one of you, took me in." He paused, a bit choked up. "You accepted me and cared about me when I wasn't worth nothin'. I treated you bad, but you just kept bein' nice." His voice broke again; he took a deep breath. "You—all of you—acted like I was part of the family. I never knew that feeling in my life, before I came here." A single tear slid down his cheek. "For the first time, I felt like someone loved me. All of you."

The whole bunch sat stunned, quiet. Then Samuel said, "We do love you, Cody." The others chimed in, sniffling and nodding.

"I made a promise to God a while back. Before I ever knew about the gold, I told Him I was gonna do something for all of you, somethin' big." Everyone was back to being speechless again, each wondering what Cody was going to say. "First thing, I ordered pews for the church building and a piano." All the women squealed with delight, and Josh and Joey jumped up shouting hallelujahs. The men laughed and clapped, shaking their heads.

Max spoke above the noise. "Cody Walton Mitchel, you just made the folks of this town very happy and grateful to God for you bringing the answer to our prayers."

Cody smiled shyly. "Well, Max, that ain't all I have ta say. The lawyer has drawn up papers like a will. Only I'm still here." He chuckled. "The money will be divided up among all of you. That's why we'll need a bank in this town."

Millie gasped. "Cody, darlin', that's mighty good of you, but your father left that gold to you."

Cody smiled. "If it'll make ya feel better, Millie, I bought a piano for Hillside Methodist too." Everyone laughed. "Besides, ma'am, you're the one that taught me to dream. And I pray all of you will figure out your dream. Maybe the money will help you get there."

Mille got up from her chair, walked to where Cody stood, and wrapped him in her arms. "I'm so proud, I could bust, son. Your bigheartedness is going to make a difference in every life here. But Cody, what about you? What about your dream?"

He kissed her on the cheek and broke into a huge smile. "That's the best part! This comin' September"—he paused and his face flushed— "This comin' September, right here in our church buildin'—and y'all better be here—I'll be marryin' Lila Penrose."

He looked at Millie, who gasped, tears threatening again. She plopped in the nearby rocker, fanning herself. The crowd was whooping it up, shouting out their congratulations.

"Just wait'll ya *meet* her!" Cody shouted above the noise.

When they had settled down, he added quietly, with somewhat mixed emotion, "Then Lila and me, we're goin' to Illinois, to seminary. My dream is to be a preacher."

You could hear a pin drop. Eventually, little Jake spoke up from the front row, sounding just like his father. "Will wonders never cease!"

———

It was a beautiful fall day. The pews were polished, the piano in place. Buckets of wildflowers—purple and blue—adorned the pulpit. The Penrose family had arrived a few weeks before, bringing Kitty with them. The folks of Thatcher Springs welcomed them all wholeheartedly, agreeing that Lila and Cody's was a match made in heaven.

Millie and Esther worked on the bridal gown; Kate, Grace, and Kitty prepared for the shindig to follow. Wade McKenzie, the new circuit preacher, was to take part in the service so Pastor Ike could walk his daughter down the aisle and then preside over the ceremony.

Millie and Silas walked hand in hand over to the church. "Ya know, Silas, it's because of you that we're here today. Because of your bein' willin' to take Cody under your wing, to be a father to him. I'm so proud of you."

Silas laughed. "Well, darlin', you're the woman behind both us men. Truth is, God just saw fit to use you and me both. And what a blessin' to see Cody's life changed. This weddin' today is the frostin' on the cake."

Cody stood waiting for his bride. He looked amazing in Max's blue coat. His normally untamed hair was combed back, a stray lock falling onto his forehead. The once ragtag hooligan had somehow become a fine-looking young man with broad shoulders, a square jaw, and tanned skin. His eyes sparkled with happiness, and at the first chord on the piano, a bright smile lit up his face.

Lila Penrose walked in, took her father's arm, and proceeded down the aisle toward him. She looked like an angel in a cloud of white lace. The fitted bodice complemented her curves and tiny waist. And the skirt, tier after tier of ruffles, flounced with each step, sunlight from the open door behind her giving it an airy look. She let her hair have its own way, with a simple tiara of pearls like a princess. Cody couldn't believe she was soon to be his wife. He knew God had truly blessed him.

Kitty, at the piano, had practiced for the past few months on the new piano at Hillside Methodist, trying to get the honky-tonk out of the hymns she was learning. Staying with the Penrose family had brought healing. She looked like a different person—her hair shinier, eyes brighter, cheeks rosier. She had gained back some weight, thanks to Esther's good cooking. The greatest change was that Kitty had invited the Lord into her heart, to be Master of her life. She was a new creature, forgiven.

She played softly until the wedding party and guests worked their way slowly out into the afternoon sun. When at last she stood and gathered her song sheets, a lone clap came from the opposite side of the pulpit, just out of her sight. To her surprise, it was the circuit preacher.

"Wonderful!" Wade exclaimed sincerely. "Where did you learn to play?"

Kitty gasped, embarrassed. "You'd never guess," she finally said.

He smiled a rather engaging smile. "Well, maybe I could try guessin' a little later on. Would you, uh, like to accompany me to the reception?"

Kitty timidly took the arm he offered, giving him a sideways glance. *For a preacher, he's mighty good to look at.*

Chapter 39

Kate pulled weeds from around the cross that marked her father's grave. She had picked a few late-blooming flowers and arranged them to place there.

Sitting back on her heels, she looked up at the early evening sky, which was mostly cloudy. "Oh, Papa, I miss you so. One day we'll be together again, but I wish I could sit on your lap right now, just for a bit. This place where we stopped so long ago, on our way to Oregon, remember? It's become home. I'll never forget the scrumptious meal Millie served us." Kate smiled at the memory. "She's been like a mother to me, Papa, a grandmother to my children. This little spot in the road has grown into home for me and Max and the finest assembly of folks you could ever hope for. We are a close-knit family. I love each one dearly. And, Papa, you would never recognize Silas. God has used that man in incredible ways."

She went on, telling him about her sisters and Grace and Sam, laughing and crying at the same time. "Oh, I'll have to tell ya about Cody and Lila next time. I see my family headin' this way." She laughed at the sight of them in the distance. "Oh my! They're ridin' Dixie, the milk cow." She giggled again and went on as if her father were right there. "Annie's up front. with Jake sitting in the middle, holding her, and Ruthie K behind Jake, holding tight to him. One of the twins is leading Dixie—can't tell which one—and Max and the other twin are walking behind."

She waved in their direction. "Oh, Papa. I'm so happy. Never in my dreams did I expect to marry a man like Max and to be blessed with adorable, incredible children. I love them all so much. Oh, and Papa, Max doesn't know yet, but we're havin' another one."

Just then the gray clouds parted for a moment, allowing a bright shaft of light to pour down on her. She sat still, gazing upward. "I love you too, Papa."

———

"Well, if that don't beat all." It was Silas sitting on the porch with his wife, enjoying an after-supper coffee.

Millie shaded her eyes against the setting sun. "Is that Dixie those Reed kids are ridin'?"

From their view, the family and the cow, a couple of dogs chasing along behind, made a perfect silhouette. They were sauntering across the way to home. Millie commenced to name each one, sure she could tell Josh and Joe apart, even from that distance.

They noticed that Max and Kate had slowed, lagging behind the parade, and then stopped. Silas and Millie leaned forward a bit, watching with curiosity. All at once, Max threw his hat in the air, let out a whoop, picked up his wife, and whirled her around in circles.

"Well, bless Pat! They're havin' another one."Silas looked at his wife, his heart bursting with love. Living with this woman, in this wide open country he loved so much, must be like heaven. — Just a little taste of heaven.